A Gangsta's Pain 2

J-Blunt

Lock Down Publications and Ca$h
Presents

A Gangsta's Pain 2
A Novel by *J-Blunt*

J-Blunt

Lock Down Publications
P.O. Box 944
Stockbridge, Ga 30281
www.lockdownpublications.com

Copyright 2022 by J-Blunt
A Gangsta's Pain 2

Lock Down Publications
Like our page on Facebook: Lock Down Publications @
www.facebook.com/lockdownpublications.ldp

Book interior design by: **Shawn Walker**
Edited by: **Tamira Butler**

Stay Connected with Us!

Text **LOCKDOWN** to 22828 to stay up-to-date with new releases, sneak peaks, contests and more...

Thank you!

Submission Guideline.

Submit the first three chapters of your completed manuscript to ldpsubmissions@gmail.com, subject line: Your book's title. The manuscript must be in a .doc file and sent as an attachment. Document should be in Times New Roman, double spaced and in size 12 font. Also, provide your synopsis and full contact information. If sending multiple submissions, they must each be in a separate email.

Have a story but no way to send it electronically? You can still submit to LDP/Ca$h Presents. Send in the first three chapters, written or typed, of your completed manuscript to:

LDP: Submissions Dept
P.O. Box 944
Stockbridge, Ga 30281

DO NOT send original manuscript. Must be a duplicate.

Provide your synopsis and a cover letter containing your full contact information.

Thanks for considering LDP and Ca$h Presents.

Acknowledgments

Here we go again! Writing these stories never gets old because I love what I do. Shout out to everybody that's been rocking with me and supporting me throughout my fight with this injustice system. It's almost over, and when I come home, we gon' ball! Pria, follow your dreams, baby. You can do anything. Robert, I'm proud of you. There is greatness inside of you. I challenge you to find it. Kay'lahni, you give me a reason to go harder. I love you. A special THANK YOU to the fans and supporters of J-Blunt. Thanks for the feedback and the reviews. I write because I love to tell stories and entertain. Connect with me on Facebook @ Author J-Blunt

J-Blunt

Prologue

Green Bay is a small town in Northeast Wisconsin known for beer and cheese. It's also home to the Super Bowl Champion Green Bay Packers football team. What most people don't know about this small Midwestern town is that some of the world's most dangerous criminals also call Green Bay home. Murderers, rapists, robbers, and drug dealers sit inside a prison just a few blocks from the legendary Lambeau Field—the 80,000-seat stadium where the Green Bay Packers play.

Green Bay Correctional Institution is one of the oldest and most violent maximum-security prisons in the United States. Beatings, stabbings, and riots are common inside the stone fortress. To keep the peace and make sure they go home every night, some of the guards turn a blind eye to gang violence. The last thing a correctional officer wants is to be the cause of an uprising, a technical term for riot, and have to call in the National Guard all because they tried to break up a fight over a 50-dollar gambling bet. When things did get serious on the inside, the prison officials would meet with the gang leaders and try to solve the problems in house. It was no secret that the gangs really ran the prisons; not the guards. It was true that the warden made the rules, but the prisoners decided what rules they wanted to follow. And in Green Bay Correctional Institution, all the movers and shakers knew that rules were made to be broken.

One of the legendary movers and shakers inside "The Bay" was Dazè Crawford. He had been in Green Bay since he was fifteen years old. Upon entry into the big house, he made a name for himself with his knuckle game. He was a little nigga, just 5'6" and 140 pounds, but he embodied the saying, "it ain't the size of the dog in the fight but the size of the fight inside the dog." He was a kid entering a man's world where nobody gave a fuck about him being a child. Dazè heard the stories about niggas getting taken advantage of and raped. The thought of a nigga taking from him or running up in his ass was terrifying. So, every time he fought, he fought with the fear of what could happen if he lost. And that fear gave him the strength, speed, and skills to beat niggas' ass that were twice his size. As Dazè got older, he also got bigger. A growth spurt combined with working out three times a day, seven days a week, turned the boy into a man. When he got ahold of the books, the knowledge turned him into a weapon. As a result, he worked his way up the Gangster Disciples hierarchy. Thirteen years later, he was a seasoned vet and number-one shot caller.

"Dazè! Slow down, fam!" Cee-Cee called.

Dazè and the two beasts walking next to him spun around at the sound of his name being called. It was mass movement, and 300 inmates were all heading to rec, so it took a moment to figure out who called his name. When he spotted Cee-Cee in the crowd, he spoke a few words to his crew.

"Hold on, y'all. Let's wait on lil' brah."

The men stepped aside and let other inmates pass.

"What's good, family?" Cee-Cee grinned, happy to see his big homie.

"You know you got it, lil' brah. 'Bout to go to rec and fuck these niggas up on this court." Dazè grinned as the men shook hands.

"I'm on the same shit. Did you see what Giannis did to the Lakers last night? He went crazy on Bron-Bron!"

"Forty-five, fifteen, and fifteen. The Greek Freak be fucking them niggas up!" Dazè laughed, simulating a crossover as the men headed up a flight of stairs.

"That's how I'm finna do these niggas at rec. If we ain't on the same team, get out the way when I come down on a fast break," Cee-Cee warned.

Dazè looked at him like he was crazy. "Nigga, what!? You betta hope we on the same team, nigga, 'cause if we ain't, I'm locking yo' ass down for even talking to me like that."

Cee-Cee accepted the challenge. "It's been a long time since I bussed yo' ass, nigga. I see I'mma have to show you that just because you bigger don't mean you better."

The men continued to talk trash as they entered the gymnasium and quickly made their way over to the basketball court. When they saw Ball and Greedy were already picking teams, Cee-Cee shook his head in frustration. He and Greedy were locked in a silent cold war over a misunderstanding with three grams of powder, and he knew Greedy wasn't going to pick him up.

"Dazè, you hooping?" Ball asked.

"Put me down!" Dazè called, changing into his sweat shorts and Nike's. "Get Cee-Cee, too."

"I already got four. You the fifth man."

"Pick me up, Greedy," Cee-Cee called as he began changing.

"Nah, I already told Ace he can run," Greedy sneered.

Cee-Cee looked around for Ace and didn't see him. "Ace ain't here. Pick me up."

"Ace went to the hole this morning," Shake announced.

Greedy looked across the gym for another player. "C'mon, Slim."

Cee-Cee mugged Greedy. "Fuck you doing, nigga? I'm playing."

"You gon' have to get next, nigga. I already got my team." Greedy smirked.

Cee-Cee got mad and began walking toward his foe. "Fuck that shit! If I ain't playing, you ain't playing, nigga."

Greedy stood his ground, ready for whatever. "Ain't no hoes over here, nigga. What's hannenin?!"

Cee-Cee drew his arm back, but Dazè grabbed him before he could swing. "Chill, lil' brah! Chill! Don't go to the hole over that bitch ass nigga."

"I'm tired of that pussy ass nigga thinking shit sweet! I'll lay his bitch ass down!" Cee-Cee yelled.

While Dazè was trying to get Cee-Cee under control, Greedy and his niggas were gathering.

"What's good, Greedy? You need some assistance?" Von asked, approaching from the sideline with four goons. Von was also a certified mover and shaker at the maximum-security prison. He was also Dazè's sworn enemy and opposition. Like Dazè, Von had gotten locked up as a youth and worked his way up the hierarchy with the Vice Lords.

"Yeah, Lord. These niggas act like they on that over this basketball shit. I been wanting to beat Cee-Cee's ass anyway," Greedy said, ready to set it off.

"Get on point!" one of Dazè's security called when he noticed Von and Greedy gathering.

When Dazè heard the warning in his man's voice, he spun around and locked eyes with Von.

"Hey! What's going on over there!?" a CO yelled.

The inmates ignored the correctional officer while sizing up each other's crew.

"What's good, Von?" Dazè asked, looking his nemesis from head to toe.

"That disrespect y'all coming with ain't gon' be tolerated, my nigga. Niggas' actions got consequences."

"Hey! If you guys aren't playing basketball, sit down!" another guard called.

Dazè glanced at the guard before giving Von his undivided attention. "How you wanna do it, my nigga?"

"Discipline yo' boy or I'mma do it for you."

"Ain't no need for a write up. We just wanna hoop."

Von shook his head, a snarl spreading across his lips. "Nah. He disrespected my brother. Bring Cee-Cee up on charges or else."

Dazè looked taken aback. "Or else what? You threatening me, nigga?"

"Nah, nigga. I don't make threats. I make promises. Discipline yo' boy or we sending it up. You the one that got parole and go home in a couple months. I don't got shit to lose. You do."

Everybody on the compound knew Dazè was being paroled in ninety days. If he got in trouble and ended up in the hole, the parole commissioner would take Dazè's parole and he would be forced to do five more years. Dazè could see the desire in Von's eyes to trick off his release. Von was sentenced to life. Freedom wasn't a possibility. And he would love nothing more than to keep Dazè locked up with him. Dazè turned to his hitters and saw the need to do violence swirling in their eyes. They were ready. TTG all day, every day. Then he thought about his grandmother. She was so happy when she found out he was coming home. He couldn't disappoint the only person that had his back since the first day he entered the system.

"Guys! Either play basketball or sit down!" the COs yelled.

Dazè nodded toward Von and smiled. "You right, boss. I got too much to lose. I'mma discipline my nigga. Y'all can have the court. Let's go, family."

Von smiled triumphantly as he watched his rivals leave the basketball court.

"Let me get at that nigga, Dazè! Please let me sweat that nigga!" Cee-Cee pleaded.

"In due time, my nigga." Dazè smiled. "Nobody ever won a war by letting the enemy know what they was about to do."

***

Two days later

Dazè paced his small cell, anticipating the door opening at any moment. The steel screwdriver burned against his hip like it had been lit on fire. Adrenaline rushed throughout his body as thoughts of the kill flooded his mind. His plan was perfect. The pass warner was one of his loyal soldiers and hooked it up so Dazè and Von would meet on the stairwell. Another one of his soldiers assured him that the door leading to the galleries behind the cells would be open. The timing had to be perfect. One minute too early or one minute too late could be the difference between Dazè spending the rest of his life in prison or going home on parole in a few months.

Clink-clank! The door sounded before sliding open.

Dazè walked quickly from the room, leaving his door open and double timing it down the tier. He was on the fourth level and his prey was on the third, so he had to hurry. He took the stairs two at a time and was happy to see the gallery door was open on the third level just like his nigga said. He slipped behind the door, partially closing it behind him, leaving enough room for him to peek out. He snatched the screwdriver from his waist and began the anxious wait.

He hadn't killed a nigga in almost ten years. Niggas in Green Bay knew not to cross that line with Dazè. Everyone except Von. Disrespect couldn't be accepted or tolerated in Dazè's mind. And since he knew Von was trying to take his freedom away, he deserved to die even more.

Dazè had been waiting for two minutes when Von rounded the corner. The gallery doors were normally locked, so Von didn't even think to look in that direction. Instead, he focused on heading down the stairs. He had just grabbed the railing when the gallery door opened and Dazè jumped out with the six-inch screwdriver. The sight of his sworn enemy with the pointed weapon scared the fuck out of Von. He was unarmed and surprised. All he could do was scream.

"Ahh—"

The screwdriver going into his throat silenced the scream. Von grabbed his neck, trying to get away, but Dazè grabbed him by the back of his shirt and drove the screwdriver into his neck several more times. Von collapsed onto the stairs as blood spewed from his neck wounds. Not wanting to leave the body in the open, Dazè dragged his dying enemy into the gallery behind the cells. After closing the door, he raced to get rid of the murder weapon and lock himself in his cell.

Chapter 1

Junior watched the clock on the wall, his eyes following the second hand as it spun round and round, counting off the minutes. He had been staring at the clock for twenty minutes while the life he had been living in Lacrosse continuously played in his mind. Just a couple of months ago he was on top of his game. A hundred G's in the safe, riding a Corvette and Lexus, a bad bitch, and a baby on the way. And now everything was slowly draining away. Steph took his money, Quitta fucked his cousin and ruined their relationship, and now he was in the emergency room praying for God to save their unborn child.

"Why God?" he questioned aloud, staring up at the ceiling.

"Mr. Stewart?"

For a moment, Junior thought God had called his name, until he looked toward the waiting room door and saw the male nurse. "Is she okay? How is the baby?" he asked, jumping to his feet.

The nurse closed his eyes and shook his head. "I'm sorry. She miscarried."

Junior let out a frustrated breath as emptiness filled his core. "Can I see her?"

"Sure. That's why I came for you. Follow me."

Sadness welled up inside of Junior as he followed the nurse down the corridor. Losing the baby was on him. If he wouldn't have killed Terrance, the Folks wouldn't have shot up Ron's house and Quitta wouldn't have lost the baby. It was all his fault.

"She's in room 3," the nurse said, pointing to the door. "Let me know if you need anything."

"Thanks," Junior mumbled before stepping into the room.

Quitta was sitting in bed, underneath the covers, with an IV in her arm. As soon as Junior saw the tears streaming down her face, it crushed him.

"I lost the baby," Quitta cried.

"It's gon' be okay," he said softly, sitting on the bed and wrapping her in his arms.

"The baby gone. I lost the baby," she sobbed.

Hearing the pain in Quitta's voice hit a nerve, forcing him to become emotional. The tears burned as they spilled down Junior's face. "It's not yo' fault. This on me. If I wouldn't have killed Terrance, them niggas wouldn't have come to Lacrosse. This one on me. I'm sorry. I didn't know it was gon' end up like this."

The young lovers held each other and mourned the loss of their unborn. A few moments later, there was a knock on the door. When it opened, two nurses walked in carrying folders.

"Ms. Ware, Can we speak with you for a moment?" one of them asked.

Quitta wiped the tears from her face, trying to gather herself. "Yes. Come in."

The nurses walked to the bedside and grabbed ahold of Quitta's hand. Their faces were sad and serious. "I'm Nurse Jackie and this is Christine. We want to let you know that we're sorry for your loss."

"We have some papers for you to fill out. We believe life starts at conception and if you want, you can name the baby."

Quitta looked to Junior, unsure of what to do. He gave the same puzzled expression.

"Are you the father?" Christine asked.

"Yeah. I'm Junior." He nodded.

"Hi, Junior. Here at Saint Mark's, we believe that all lives matter, even the ones that are cut short because of miscarriage. We want all parents to keep the memory of their unborn alive, which is why we give you the opportunity to give it a name. Did you want a boy or a girl?"

"A girl," Quitta answered for him.

"What would you like to name her?"

"Abrianna," Quitta answered, giving the unborn one of the names she and Junior talked about.

"That's a pretty name. You can write it on this birth certificate and you and Junior can sign it," Jackie said, giving Quitta the pen and birth certificate.

After a few more instructions and giving Quitta release papers, the nurses wished them well before allowing them to leave. "Where you wanna go?" Junior asked as they walked across the parking lot.

"I'm going wherever you go."

Junior didn't respond until they were in the car. "I'm going to my mother's house. Don't you think you should go by yo' mom's house?"

Quitta spun to face him, hurt and anger in her eyes. "For real, Junior!? We just lost our fucking baby and you just gon' kick me to the curb like I'm some punk ass bitch?! Like I ain't shit. For real?"

Junior let out a breath as he pressed the start button. "Why we still going through this, Quitta? Lacrosse is done. We going back to Milwaukee to start over from scratch. We not together no more."

"What the fuck you mean we not together? You not about to leave me, nigga. Not after everything that we just went through. I just lost a baby, nigga! You said it was your fault. How the fuck you gon' leave after that? You expect me to just forgive you for fucking Nyla and giving me an STD, but I fuck Lo-Dog and now it's the end of the world. What You did to me is way worse than what I did to you. I didn't burn you, nigga. I didn't put your life or health at risk. I did you how you did me."

Junior didn't respond, just focused his attention on driving. As much as he didn't want to admit it, Quitta had a point. Not only did he fuck Nyla, he also had a threesome, got burnt, and brought a disease home. But despite his wrongs, he still couldn't get past her fucking his cousin. That shit was evil.

"You don't got nothing to say?" Quitta asked.

"I know fucking Nyla was wrong, but I'mma nigga. Niggas fuck just to fuck. That shit didn't mean nothing. You was locked up and she was there and I wanted to buss a nut. You fucking Lo-Dog was personal. You plotted against me. You betrayed me and did that shit to hurt me. What you did was scandalous as fuck. That shit was payback. I don't fuck with nobody that will plot revenge on me. When somebody want revenge, ain't no telling how far they would go to get back. You can't never trust a muthafucka that wanna get even. I don't feel like I can trust you, and I ain't feeling that shit."

Even though Quitta wanted to win the argument and get her man back, she knew that nothing she said could overcome the words he had just spoken. Junior's words were so real that Quitta was stuck.

"Damn, baby. I didn't think about it like that," Quitta confessed, her voice losing some of the anger and edge. "My mama taught me to get even with anybody that fucked me over. Even the Bible says an eye for an eye. But I never thought about how the person I got revenge on would feel. I only thought about my feelings. I didn't realize how deep that shit goes."

"That's why I feel how I feel. That shit cut a nigga too deep. I know they say 'hell hath no fury like a woman scorned,' but damn, I didn't know that shit was gon' fuck me up like that."

Quitta reached out to grab his arm. "I'm sorry, Junior."

He nodded.

"I'm for real. I don't want you thinking that I will do something evil to you, because I wouldn't. When I found out you fucked Nyla, I was devastated. I wanted to hurt you back, but I didn't think it was going to get this deep. I thought I was gon' teach you a lesson and we was gon' move on with our lives. I didn't think that I was gon' be the one being taught a lesson. But now I know how you feel about revenge, and I swear I won't ever plot against you again. I love you. You the only nigga I ever loved and I don't want to be without you. I want me, you, and Mooka to be a family. And maybe we can even have another baby as a promise that we won't ever betray each other again. I'm sorry. Can you forgive me, please?"

Junior shook his head before glancing toward the passenger seat. Quitta continued to hold his hand, looking at him through sad and regretful eyes. She was his first and only love. The only woman besides his mother and sisters that could really hurt him. The power she held over him made her dangerous. She was his weakness. He would never truly be strong until he could overcome the power she held over him. And what made her more dangerous was the fact that she had already figured out everything he was thinking.

"I know you still love me." She smiled. "You may not trust me, but I know you love me. Your eyes don't lie."

Junior turned his attention back to the road. "I'm staying at my momma house. Where you going?"

"I already told you that I'm going wherever you go," she yawned. "I'm tired. Wake me up when we get to Milwaukee."

***

Junior didn't pull up to his mother's house until almost 11 o'clock at night. He could hear Assassin barking as he stuck his key in the front door. When it opened, the German Shepard jumped up on him happily.

"Hey, girl! Move so I can come in."

"Daddy! Mama!" Mooka yelled, rushing his parents.

"What's good, young money?!" Junior smiled, moving the dog and lifting his son into his arms while looking around the living room. His grandmother, aunt, and some of his cousins were all sitting around the living room. There was also lots of extra furniture from his grandmother's house crowded into the living room.

"Hey, Grandson!" Ulebell grinned, showing off a toothless smile. Ulebell was a big boned, sixty-five-year-old woman born in Mississippi, but she moved to Wisconsin as a child because her parents wanted to escape the racism of the south.

"Hey, Granny. What y'all doing over here?" Junior asked, passing Mooka to Quitta before hugging his grandmother.

"Our house burned down about a week ago. Gail letting us stay here until we find a house. How you doing? Ain't seen you in forever."

"I'm good, Granny. We moved out of town for a lil' minute, but we back now."

"Geeoorrggee! What's hannen, boy?"

Junior turned toward the hallway and saw Ulebell's son, who was also his sister Renae's father.

"Tolou, what's up, nigga?" he smiled, hugging his sister's dad.

"Shit. I was in here kicking it with Gail until I heard yo' ass. How you been, boy?"

"I'm good. We moving back from Lacrosse. I didn't know y'all was here."

"Yeah. House burned down. We should be out of here in a couple weeks."

"Why he call you George?" Quitta asked.

Junior laughed. "Man, Tolou gave me that name when I was a shorty."

"'Cause he used to look like that lil' monkey Curious George when he was little. Geeoorrggee!" Tolou laughed.

"Hey, son and daughter!" Gail sang, coming from her room to give out hugs.

"Hey, Mama."

After Gail hugged Quitta, she stepped back to give her a head-to-toe look. "Why you wearing hospital clothes, daughter?"

Quitta looked to Junior before explaining, "We had a miscarriage."

Gail's eyes grew wide as full moons. "You was pregnant and you lost the baby!?"

Quitta nodded.

"Oh, my god! I'm so sorry to hear that!" Gail said, wrapping her in a hug.

Suddenly, everybody in the living room got up and wrapped Quitta and Junior in a big ass, loving family hug.

"What happened? Did you get sick? How did you lose the baby?" Aunty Theresa asked.

"I tripped and fell hard."

"I'm sorry to hear that. But y'all young. Y'all can have lots more babies. Practice makes perfect," Ulebell laughed.

"How long y'all in town for?" Gail asked.

"We back for good. Didn't work out in Lacrosse like we wanted it to," Junior explained.

Gail looked surprised. "Oh. Well, I gave your room to your sister. Everybody sleeping wherever they lay they head at. Y'all can stay if y'all don't got nowhere to go."

"We'll figure it out."

20

Junior and Quitta hung out with the family until everyone started getting ready for bed. Realizing there wasn't enough room at his mother's house for their family, Junior and Quitta decided their next best plan was Quitta's mother's house. But that move would have to wait until the morning because Darlene didn't open her door after 10:00 at night. Since they only had a couple hundred dollars to their name, they planned to spend the night in the hotel. After getting their son dressed and saying bye, they hopped in the Lexus truck. Junior pressed the button, but the truck didn't start.

"Shit!" he cursed.

"What's wrong?" Quitta asked.

"It won't start," Junior said, pressing the button again. The truck still didn't start.

"This been a fucked-up day," Quitta breathed, shaking her head.

Junior lay his head against the headrest and closed his eyes. "Man, I can't think of a day that's been worse than this. Let's just spend the night here and figure it out in the morning."

"Where we gon' sleep?" Quitta asked. "It's ten people in that house and four bedrooms."

"We can go upstairs and make a palette on the floor. It's just for one night."

Nobody spoke for a moment. When Junior opened his eyes, Quitta was watching him. "What?"

She was about to say something but stopped. "I'm going wherever you go."

Junior took his family back inside. After explaining the situation to his mom, he grabbed some blankets and took Quitta and Mooka upstairs. After making a pallet on the floor in Renae's new room/his old room, they lay down. Junior closed his eyes but couldn't sleep. He just lay there, losing track of time as the life he lived in Lacrosse for the last few months played in his head. He couldn't believe he had gone from being a have to a have not. From a hundred thousand dollars to a couple hundred dollars. Couldn't believe that life had brought him to sleeping on the floor with his family. He didn't have a pot to piss in or a window to throw it out of. And now that the truck was broke, he didn't have enough money to fix it. Not only was he homeless, but they also didn't have a car. He felt like a failure. Less of a man.

"You still woke?" Quitta asked.

Junior opened his eyes and looked toward his baby mama. She lay on the floor next to him, her brown eyes glowing in the pale moonlight that was shining through the window. "Yeah. I can't sleep. You good?"

"Yeah. My stomach hurt a little, but I'm good. What's wrong with you? How come you can't sleep?"

Junior's eyes rested on Mooka for a moment. The toddler slept peacefully between his parents. Mooka didn't have a care in the world. As far as the child knew, life was good. He was sleeping next to his mom and dad, surrounded by a house filled with family members. Junior envied his son at that moment. How he wished life could be so simple.

"I feel like a failure," Junior admitted, closing his eyes so Quitta wouldn't see the emotions threatening to spill. "Everything in our life is fucked up right now, and I feel like it's all my fault. I'm your man and Mooka's father, so I'm responsible for how y'all live. Right now we at the bottom, and I don't know how we got here or how I'mma get us out of this shit."

Quitta reached out and touched her man's face. "Look at me, baby."

Junior's eyelids parted slowly, revealing eyes filled with tears that refused to spill.

Seeing the pain in her man's eyes touched Quitta, making her eyes misty. "We in this thing called life together, baby daddy. Remember when we was riding in the car the first day you got out and I told you that everything I wanted was in the car? I meant that. Being with you and Mooka is all that matters. It don't matter if we rich and driving foreign or sleeping on the floor at yo' mama's house. The only thing I care about is us being together, because I know that together we are more than enough. Whatever we had, I know we can get it back. You a strong man and I love you, and I got your back. This is temporary. You can't keep a real nigga down."

Quitta's words were like a cool towel laid across a burning wound. Her belief in him and his ability to rise above anything was inspirational. "Damn, baby mama. You don't know how bad I needed to hear that."

"I know." She smiled before moving in for a kiss.

"My moms told me that behind every strong nigga is a stronger woman. I finally get it now. I need you to be my rock, Quitta. When I'm slipping, I need you to get me back on track. I'mma get us up off this floor, that's my word."

"I know what you need. I know my role. I'm your backbone, baby. Your ride or die. Us against the world."

J-Blunt

Chapter 2

"Junior, get up, nigga!"

Junior and Quitta opened their eyes and saw John standing in the middle of the room holding Mooka.

"John, what's good, nigga?" Junior yawned, sitting up and stretching the kinks out of his body from sleeping on the hard floor. "Shit. Mama said y'all was up here. What's up, Quitta? You look like yo' breath stank," he cracked.

"Fuck you, nigga!" Quitta cursed before throwing her shoe at him. "What's up, though? Where you was at last night? Gail said you gotta girlfriend now."

"It ain't shit." John blushed. "Just a lil' something I was doing. I couldn't stay here with all these muthafuckas so I moved in with shorty."

"On what, you fucking with big booty Nicole though?" Junior asked. "Stepped yo' game up with that one, boy."

John got arrogant. "Nah, nigga. She stepped her game up fucking with me. I'm the catch. I'm putting on for dark-skinned niggas. Tyrese went crazy, so now I'm doing it all by myself."

"Fool ass nigga!" Quitta laughed.

"You gon' play the game with me, Uncle John?" Mooka asked.

"Let's get down later, my nigga. Right now I need to holla at yo' pops," John said before sitting the toddler down and turning to Junior. "Get up, brah. Let me get a ride to the store so I can grab some wraps."

"The truck broke down last night, nigga."

John looked surprised. "On what?! Damn, that's why you at moms house sleeping on the floor, huh?"

Junior shook his head before sliding into his shoes. "Man, so much shit happened to us over the last couple days. Let's mob to the store and get lifted. Baby, you want something from the store?" he asked Quitta.

"Get some cigarettes and something to drink. And grab something for Mooka."

"I want some candy, Daddy!" Mooka yelled excitedly.

"I got you, man," Junior said before turning to John. "Let's mob."

"Y'all moving back to Milwaukee?" John asked as they walked through the Parklawn Housing Projects.

Junior let out a stressed breath. "Yeah. We don't got no choice. Couple days ago, I had to off a nigga and his niggas came back with that drama. Damn near pushed my shit back. Bitch ass niggas had that heat. Monkey nuts and drums on they shit. Made Quitta have a miscarriage."

John's eyes grew wide with surprise. "Brah, Quitta lost the baby!? And you had to off a nigga!?"

Junior nodded. "Hell yeah. Bitch ass nigga Terrance tried to hoe me. I put that shit in his face. The Folks came from Chicago and tried to get me out the way. Ron said they gotta green light on me. The nigga Terrance was plugged in."

John's eyes grew even wider. "The Folks gotta hit out on you, nigga!?"

Junior shrugged. "I guess."

"What the fuck!? Did you tell Six?"

"Not yet. I'm still try'na figure this shit out."

"Damn, nigga. Do they know where you from? Do they know where Mama live?"

"I don't think so. But that ain't even all of it. This bitch ass nigga, Steph, hit me for a hunnit and half a book. I'm fucked up. All we got is the clothes on our back. Probably can't even get the truck fixed. And I gotta Corvette all the way up in Lacrosse stuck in storage."

John looked at Junior like he stank. "You let a nigga take yo shit, brah?"

Junior returned the look that John gave him. "God ain't made a nigga bad enough to take shit from me. This was Quitta's ex. She was fucking with the nigga while I was locked up. When I touched down, she called the police on that nigga and gave me his line and money. He got out while we was fucking with Six in Nevada and broke in the house. Hit it outta town with my shit."

John shook his head. "Damn, my nigga. Y'all went through a lot of shit. And sis a fool for getting the nigga knocked and giving you his shit. She cold."

"What else she was gon' do? Daddy came back home and she knew she couldn't come back empty handed. Real boss shit, young nigga," Junior bragged.

John nodded. "That was some player shit. Real talk. But what you on now? I know y'all ain't finna stay with Mama while Grams n'em up in there."

"Hell nah. I ain't finna be sleeping on the floor no more. Probably stay with Quitta's moms 'til I get right."

The brothers were silent for a moment.

"What about Quitta?" John asked.

Junior looked at John and saw the real question in his eyes. Quitta fucked their cousin. Was he still going to fuck with her even though she crossed that line?

"What about her?" Junior asked, trying to evade the question.

"She fucked Lo-Dog. The whole family know. Lotta niggas got a lot of shit to say about that. You gon' accept that?"

"Man, John..." Junior breathed. "I don't know what to do, my nigga. Quitta my bitch. She will thug for a nigga. Get it out the mud with me. But fucking Lo-Dog was too much. She say she did it to pay me back for fucking Nyla. I don't know what to do."

"You can't reward a bitch for being disloyal, brah. I love Quitta like a sister, but she did too much. Certain shit that a mu'fucka shouldn't be forgiven for."

"I hear you, my nigga. Shit complicated," Junior said before going quiet.

The brothers walked in silence for a moment.

"You really in love with her, huh?" John asked.

Junior looked over and saw a seriousness in his little brother's eyes. It wasn't a judgmental question but a serious one.

"For real, for real. I'mma sucka, on what?"

John laughed. "Yeah, you definitely a sucka. But that's what love make a nigga do. And that's why I'm scared of that shit. I can't let no bitch get me in my fag body. But you my big bro and I fuck

27

with you. You gon' always be my nigga, no matter what. But what about Lo-Dog?"

"What about him?" Junior asked.

"You forgave him too?"

"I don't fuck with cuz like that. He bogus," Junior snarled.

"So is Quitta, but you forgave her. Plus, he blood. I know you ain't finna forgive her and not cuz. That's some real sucka shit."

"Well, I'mma be a sucka then. Fuck Lo-Dog," Junior mugged. "We ain't family no more and I'm through talking about that nigga."

***

"Damn, lil' nigga. You telling me that a nigga really took a hunnit thousand dollars from you?" Fifty asked.

They were sitting in his living room smoking while watching *American Gangster*. Junior wanted to talk about getting some money, but all Fifty wanted to talk about was the loss.

"He didn't take shit from me. He broke in the house while we was out of town."

"Same shit. Where the nigga from? Where his family at?"

"That nigga from out east. New York or some shit. He gone. But I ain't try'na keep talking about that shit. Ain't nothing I can do about it."

"What about Quitta fucking Lo-Dog though? I heard about that shit and I was tripping, like whhaatt!"

Junior mugged Fifty. "C'mon, my nigga. I ain't try'na talk about none of that depressing ass shit. I fucked her family and she fucked mine. That shit over. What's up with some paper though? I'm fucked up. I need to get my bag right. I gotta get my car fixed and get the fuck outta Quitta's mama's house."

Fifty gave Junior a long searching look. "So, can anybody fuck Quitta since you gon' forgive her? Remember, I asked first." Junior mugged his long-time friend and big homie, damn near ready to fight.

Fifty bust out laughing. "I'm just fucking with you, my nigga. Chill. Look like you wanna try me. I'm just bullshitting."

Junior shook his head. "You play too much, nigga. That shit ain't funny. What's up with a move, though? I need to hit a lick."

"I been plotting on a nigga for a minute. Bitch ass nigga, Fredo. But you know how I like to move. Sic a bitch on 'em and let her open the door."

"Oh, yeah. Like we did Vel. Where Lisa? Sic that bitch on his ass."

Fifty shook his head. "Lisa gone."

Junior waited for Fifty to explain more, but he didn't. "Where she at?"

"Bitch threatened to tell on me, so I laid her ass down."

Junior's eyes grew wide. "You whacked yo' bitch?!"

Fifty gave a serious look. "I don't play them type of bitch ass games, my nigga. Ain't nobody finna threaten me with sending me to jail or getting me killed by my enemies. I'll shoot my daddy for that shit."

Junior was at a momentary loss for words. "A'ight. I feel you, my nigga. I ain't finna let nobody get me smoked or put me back in Dodge. So, how you wanna hit this nigga? What else can we do?"

Fifty held Junior's eyes for a moment. "Use Quitta."

Junior laughed. "Yeah right."

Fifty continued to stare at him.

"You serious?" Junior asked.

"We moving on short notice. Plus, we need a bad bitch. That nigga gon' go for Quitta. No lie. Plus, she gotta prove her loyalty for fucking the fam. Quitta is perfect, my nigga."

***

"Hey, Mama Darlene." Junior smiled, greeting his second mother as he stepped into the house.

"Hey, son-in-law! How you doing, baby?" she asked, opening her arms for a hug. Quitta's mother was a beautiful and curvy brown-skinned woman that loved Jesus and sipping on Jesus Juice.

"I'm good. I was gon' ask how you doing, but that strawberry daiquiri you holding telling me everything I need to know."

"Amen!" She smiled, taking a sip. "Lock the door and come talk to Mama for a minute. Quitta and Mooka went to the store with Stanley. They should be back in a minute."

After locking the door, Junior sat on the couch across from Darlene. "What's going on, Ma?"

"Quitta told me about the miscarriage and how you feel it was your fault."

Junior lowered his head for a moment before meeting the older woman's gaze. "Yeah. They shot up Ron's house because of something I did. If I wouldn't have done what I did, they wouldn't have shot up the house."

She nodded. "You might be right about that. I remember when my son house got shot up, but I didn't know you had something to do with it. Yeah, maybe if you hadn't done whatever you did, they wouldn't have shot up the house. But that don't mean that Quitta still wouldn't have had the miscarriage. God allowed that to happen for a reason, and the one thing that I know is that nobody can change the will of God. We might get mad at God and say it's not fair. That's our prerogative. But the thing is, son, we can't think like God. God is not a man and He don't think like we do. Sometimes things don't make sense to us because they ain't supposed to. Man is finite. God is infinite. We can't think like Him. You know what I'm saying?"

Junior nodded. "I read the Bible while I was locked up and I heard that before. But I still don't understand why God allows bad stuff to happen to people. I thought God was supposed to be righteous?"

"He is righteous, baby. God is so good! There is so much more to God than you know. And I know it don't make sense right now, but when the time is right, God might reveal it to you. God is perfect. He don't make mistakes. I just wanted to tell you that so you don't go around thinking that the miscarriage was your fault. Sometimes bad things happen. That's just the way of life."

Junior thought on her words for a moment. "I hear you, Ma. Definitely gave me something to think about."

"That's the point. To make you think." Darlene smiled. "My glass getting empty. You want me to make you a drink?"

"Yeah. Show me how to make one of those. Look like it taste good."

While Darlene was teaching Junior the fine art of daiquiri making, Quitta walked in the house with Mooka and her stepfather, Stanley.

"Junior, what's up, nigga!?" Stanley smiled.

"What's good, Stan-the-Man?" Junior nodded. "Moms teaching me how to make a daiquiri."

"A daiquiri?" Stanley frowned. "Man, don't be messing with them fruity drinks. We men. We drink it straight," he said before grabbing the bottle of vodka from the table and taking a drink. "That's how a man do it, baby boy!"

"A man can drink a fruity drink too, Stanley. You like long island ice tea. That's fruity," Darlene said.

Stanley gave her a look. "You giving me some lip, woman?"

Darlene returned the look, resting both hands on her wide hips. "Who you think you talking to like that, sucka?"

Stanley broke into a grin. "C'mon, baby. You know I'm just playing. See, Junior. You done got me in trouble, nigga."

Junior lifted his hands. "What I do?"

"Nothing, baby," Darlene said, passing him the freshly made fruity drink. "Every now and then I gotta remind him that the man wears the pants but the skirt is more powerful."

Junior laughed at Stanley before grabbing his drink and going to find his woman. She and Mooka were in their bedroom. Quitta was sitting on the bed going through shopping bags.

"Hey, Daddy! Look at my toy Grandad bought me!" Mooka said, showing off his new action figure.

"Oh yeah, man! That's slick," Junior said before plopping down on the bed next to Quitta. "Hey, baby? What's in the bags?"

"Some hygiene stuff for us and some sweat suits. We don't got no clothes, so I had to get us something to wear. By the way, we broke now. Let me have some of that."

Junior took one more drink from the daiquiri before handing it to Quitta. "I figured out a way to fix our broke problem."

Quitta gave him her undivided attention. "How?"

"We gon' have to take it. And we need your help."

She frowned. "What you talking about? And who is we?"

"We gotta lay a nigga down. You, me, and Fifty."

Quitta's eyes grew wide. "You want me to help y'all rob somebody? And why you still fucking with Fifty? He the reason you got locked up already."

"C'mon, Quitta. That's my nigga. And we need some money so we can get the fuck outta yo' mama house. This the fastest way I know."

Quitta wasn't sold. "I don't want to do it. Plus, you already got locked up fucking with him. Why not just call Six? He got money. Tell him to put you back on."

"This how I used to get it before. Except this a one-time thing. And I ain't finna be calling my brother every time I'm fucked up. I'm my own man. You said you my ride or die. Us against the world. Trust yo' nigga, baby. Just do this one time and then we going to the moon."

Quitta studied Junior's face for a long moment. She could see the promise of better days in his eyes. He needed help, and she couldn't turn him down. Even if it was the wrong play, she had to ride with her man.

"Okay, baby daddy. What you want me to do?"

Junior smiled.

***

Kinky's was a newly opened club on Milwaukee's north side. If you had a couple dollars and wanted to have a good time in a chill atmosphere, Kinky's was the spot to be. The bar served everything from tap beer to top shelf, and the DJ played music that kept the dance floor packed. If dancing wasn't your thing, there was also a section with a couple pool tables and dart boards.

A Gangsta's Pain 2

Junior walked in the club on a mission. He was dressed simply in a black Ksubi T-shirt, black Ksubi jeans, a black cap, and a pair of black Gucci loafers. Compared to the flashy niggas in the club that wore Fendi, Louis Vuitton, and Amiri and rocked ice shined with fifty pointers, Junior might as well had been invisible. And that's exactly what he wanted. To not be seen.

Quitta, on the other hand, was shining like a diamond-studded Richard Millie. She wore a little shadow to bring out her eyes and shiny lip gloss with gold flakes that made her lips bling in the lights. Her hot pink lace-front wig matched the hot pink Ms. Cat bodysuit that showed every curve of her perfectly sculpted body. Her nipples forced their way through the thin fabric across her chest, and her pussy lips looked like they were chewing the fabric between her thighs. The white open-toe Prada heels had her ass sitting up like she got shots, bouncing every time she took a step. Every nigga and female that she walked by were forced to look at the twenty piece that could easily demand a million followers on Instagram.

"You killing it, baby," Junior admitted, leading his woman to the bar. "Celebrity status."

"I don't like that everybody looking at me. I mean, normally I'm cool with it, but tonight I don't like it. I'm standing out too much. What if they remember me?"

"That's the point, baby. You need to stand out so he notices you. Do you see him?" Junior asked, looking around inconspicuously.

"Not yet."

When they got to the bar, Junior ordered them double shots of XO and beers. The predators downed the shots and sipped the brews while looking for their prey.

"I see him," Quitta said, nodding toward a table near the wall on the other side of the club.

Junior followed her line of sight and smiled. Fredo was a dark-skinned, bald-headed, fat nigga with big lips and a big pot belly. He was also eating. The carats in his ears, iced-out BGM chain, and Rolex on his wrist testified that he was getting to it. He was dressed in designer drip, looking like a lick. He was also surrounded by a squad of niggas that matched his look. No matter who Quitta tempted, it was going to be a nice payday.

"C'mon. Let's dance so you can get these niggas attention," Junior said.

Lakeya and Yung Bleu's song "Perfect" was playing as they stepped onto the dance floor. Junior played the part of an awkward and lame nigga that didn't have rhythm. Quitta danced on and all around him while they moved closer to Fredo's table. It didn't take long for Quitta to get the mark's attention. When they made eye contact, Quitta made sure to let her stare linger before turning her attention back to Junior.

"He looking at me, baby," she whispered in Junior's ear.

"Show out."

When Quitta looked at Fredo again, she saw he was still watching her. She licked her lips and smiled before turning around and shaking her phatty. Junior humped against her ass awkwardly, keeping his back to Fredo and his niggas. When Quitta spun around to face Fredo again, he was laughing and pointing at Junior's back. Then he gave a nod before lifting his hands and waving her over. Quitta smiled again before turning her attention back to Junior. They continued to dance, the whole time Quitta and Fredo making gestures behind Junior's back. After a couple of songs, they moved to a table to catch a chill. Quitta made sure to sit facing Fredo.

"He on my heels, baby daddy. This nigga ready to go," Quitta said, sneaking peeks at the iced-out fat nigga.

"I'm finna use the bathroom and get some drinks. Get him to come over," Junior said before heading to the bathroom.

Quitta eyed Fredo. He was watching Junior. As soon as Junior walked in the restroom, Fredo made his move.

"You know you the baddest muthafucka up in here, right?" Fredo asked as he approached the table.

"Thank you." Quitta blushed. "I'm just try'na have a good time, but this nigga ain't who I thought he was. Got me drinking beer n'shit."

Fredo laughed. "C'mon, shorty. Come fuck with me and my niggas. Top shelf all night. Leave this bum ass nigga and come fuck with a nigga that really run the city."

Quitta looked unsure. "I don't wanna do him like that. He a nice person. Plus, I don't even know you."

"I'm BGM Fredo. I know you heard of Bread Gang Mafia. We fucking up the city."

Recognition flashed in Quitta's eyes. "Yeah, I heard of y'all. I seen some of y'all videos."

"You already know what we about then. What's yo' name?"

"I'm Lana," she lied.

"Check it out, Lana. If you wanna have a good time, come to my table. You can't have a good time if you ballin' on a budget. Fuck with me, you know I got it."

Quitta still looked unsure. "I don't know."

Fredo looked toward the bar and made eye contact with Junior. He was heading back to the table with two more beers.

"Well, you gon' have to make yo' mind up quick 'cause yo' man on the way back. And he got more beers," Fredo laughed.

Quitta pretended to be scared when she saw Junior. "Awe shit!"

"What the fuck is this!?" Junior snapped, slamming the drinks on the table. "I leave for one minute and you entertaining other niggas? Who the fuck is this?" he yelled, pointing at Fredo.

"Wait, man!" Quitta said, standing up. "He just walked over here. It ain't like that."

Junior turned his aggression on Fredo. "What the fuck you want, nigga? This my girl. What's good?"

Fredo laughed. "That's yo' girl?"

"That's what I just said, nigga."

Fredo sucked his teeth. "Listen, my nigga. She ain't feeling you. Real shit. She don't even like beer, family. I don't think you know what to do with something like that. Let me take her off yo' hands."

"What, nigga!?" Junior mugged, moving like he was about to throw a punch, but Quitta stepped in front of him.

"Hold on, man! Don't do this. Let me talk to you for a minute."

Fredo took a step back and reached for his waist. "You betta listen to shorty for' you get fucked over, fuck boy!"

"Oh, it's like that!" Junior mugged. "You know what, Lana? Fuck you and fuck that nigga, too! I'm out this bitch," Junior said before storming away.

"Wait, man! Hold on!" Quitta said, giving chase.

They continued to have a fake argument all the way to the parking lot. When they got to the Malibu, they lowered their voices. "We about to change cars and I'm coming right back. You need to be out of there in twenty minutes," Junior instructed.

"Okay. I got it. I'm scared, but I got it."

Junior wanted to comfort Quitta but couldn't. He wasn't sure who was watching and they had to be quick.

"Bitch, get the fuck out my face. Go back in there with that nigga!" Junior snapped before climbing in the Malibu where Fifty was waiting.

Quitta turned around and headed back to the club.

"How it go?" Fifty asked.

"She got that nigga." Junior smiled.

***

When Quitta walked back inside the bar, she made her way to Fredo. He was happy to see her again.

"Lana! That's what I'm talking about. Leave that bitch nigga and fuck with a rich nigga!"

Quitta pretended to be mad. "That bitch ass nigga tried to hit me. Ooh, I wanna fuck him up."

"Baby, don't get mad. Get money. Come fuck with yo' boy. These my BGM niggas. Let's have a drink and kick it. Show you how bosses do it."

Quitta went to the table and kicked it with the ballers. After twenty minutes, she got Fredo's attention. "Hey, can you take me home?"

Fredo frowned. "Home!? You only been here for a couple minutes. I thought you came out for a good time."

"I did, but that nigga killed my vibe and I kinda feel like I'm in the way. I just ain't feeling it."

"Okay, okay. Say less. I got you," he said before turning to his niggas. "Aye, I'm about to move with shorty. I'mma fuck with you niggas later."

"Let me know what that pussy taste like!" one of the BGM niggas called as they walked away.

When they were outside, Fredo walked her to an all-black Grand Wagoneer.

"Damn, this a big ass truck," Quitta commented as she climbed in the passenger seat.

"This that new shit by Jeep. A Wagoneer. Gotta have a big truck for a big nigga. Where you try'na go? I gotta spot not too far from here if you wanna kick it some more."

"I think you a cool nigga and I like yo' vibe, but I'm not try'na do nothing extra tonight. But I do wanna kick it with you. We can exchange numbers and get together another time."

"For sure. For sure. Tell me where you try'na go."

"I left my car by this nigga house, on 35th and Silver Spring. Can you take me to it?"

"For sure, baby. Lay back and chill."

Quitta pretended to be into Fredo as they got to know each other while he drove. When they pulled up to the empty Malibu, Quitta was happy that her part of the mission was over.

"This is me right here," she said, ready to get the hell out of the truck.

"A'ight, shorty. I'mma call you tomorrow, a'ight? I'mma have something set up for us to do. Cool?" Fredo asked.

"I like that. Make sure you call," Quitta said before climbing from the truck and getting in Fifty's car.

When the big SUV pulled away, a Ford Escape pulled out behind it. Even though Quitta couldn't see who was in the SUV, she already knew Fifty and Junior were inside. Her phone began to vibrate. It was a text from Junior.

'You did good. Meet me at Mama house.'

***

Fifty drove the Ford truck through traffic, staying a half block from the Wagoneer. The plan was to follow him home and run inside.

"What this nigga doing?" Junior asked as the black SUV turned into the gas station.

"This might be the perfect opportunity. We can catch him while he pumping gas," Fifty said. "I'mma park around back. Get 'em, nigga."

Junior put on the black COVID-19 mask. "Say less."

When Fifty stopped the Escape, Junior hopped out and walked quickly around to the front of the gas station. Fredo was just coming out of the gas station, walking to the truck. He was looking through his phone with his head down. Slipping. Junior timed it perfectly. As soon as Fredo climbed in the truck, Junior opened the passenger door and pointed the 357 Taurus in his chest.

"Be easy, my nigga. Let's take a ride."

Fredo froze when he saw the gun. "What you on, nigga?"

"Start the truck and drive. Take me to the safe."

Fredo was stuck for a moment, unsure of what to do. When he looked in Junior's eyes, recognition shown. "That was you at the club?"

Junior let out a chuckle. "Drive, Fredo. Make this easy. You know you can make that shit back."

Fredo shook his head, biting his bottom lip. "I can't believe this bitch ass shit!"

"Let's go, nigga. Start the truck," Junior demanded.

Fredo shook his head. "Nah. We ain't going nowhere. It's fifty racks in the console. Take that shit and get the fuck out my truck."

Junior looked toward the console but didn't move. "Drive, nigga. If I gotta say it again, I'mma make you bleed."

Fredo mugged Junior before pressing the start button. He threw the truck in drive and stomped on the gas pedal. The big truck jumped forward as the engine revved, making Junior fall back into the seat. Then Fredo hit the brakes, jerking the truck to a stop. Junior flew into the dashboard, accidentally squeezing the trigger and firing a shot. Before he could gather himself, Fredo dove at him, grabbing the gun. Not only did the fat nigga have the advantage with the element of surprise, but he also had a weight advantage. While Junior was trying to make sure he kept the gun, Fredo was climbing further into the passenger seat, smothering Junior with his big body.

Pop, pop, pop! The gun fired, sending bullets through the windshield.

"I'mma kill you with yo' own gun, bitch ass nigga!" Fredo grinned, pushing his elbow into Junior's throat as he climbed on top of him.

Junior was struggling to breath because the fat nigga was sitting on top of him with his elbow on his throat. Fredo also had both of his hands on the 357 and was twisting it from Junior's hand. Junior knew when Fredo took the gun, he was dead. Quitta and Mooka's faces flashed in his mind. Darlene's words about God allowing things to happen to people played in his head. God was about to allow him to die.

Pop!

Junior flinched as blood and brains sprayed on his face and Fredo collapsed on top of him.

"Junior, you good, nigga?!" Fifty asked.

"Yeah. Help me get this fat ass nigga off me," he breathed, happy to be alive.

"How the fuck you let this nigga get on top of you?" Fifty asked as they threw the fat nigga on the ground.

"Bitch ass nigga hit the gas and brakes and slammed me into the dashboard," Junior said as he wiped blood from his face. "He said it's fifty in the console. Grab that shit."

Fifty opened the center console and pulled out the money. "Got it! Let's go."

"I gotta take this truck. We gotta set it on fire. Look at my fingerprints."

Junior's bloody prints were all over the dashboard and seat.

"You drive. Follow me," Fifty said before running to the Ford.

The trucks sped from the gas station, leaving Fredo's dead body near the gas pump.

Chapter 3

Quitta waited nervously in the Malibu, looking in all directions for a sign of Junior. She was scared as hell. The plans changed. She was supposed to go home and wait for Junior but when she got the text to meet him on 29th and Villard, she knew something was wrong. So she sat, going over in her mind what could have gone wrong. Did Junior get hurt? Did he have a run-in with the police? Did Fredo figure out that she set him up? Her mind ran a million miles an hour until she saw two figures emerge from a yard a few houses away. She knew it was Junior by the way he walked. Fifty was next to him. The racing of her mind and heart slowed when she saw he was safe.

"You okay, baby?" Quitta asked when he climbed in the passenger seat.

"I'm good."

"I guess I don't matter," Fifty cracked as he climbed in the backseat.

"It ain't like that. I'm glad that both of y'all okay. Where we going? And why y'all smell like fire?"

"We good," Junior repeated. "Take us home."

"What happened? I thought you was supposed to meet me at home? Did you get the money?"

Junior remained tight lipped. "We gon' talk about it later. Just get us home."

Quitta knew not to ask any more questions. Something bad happened and the men weren't going to talk about it. Instead of pestering them with more questions, she focused on getting them home safe. When they pulled up to her mother's house, she said bye to Fifty and went in the house. Junior lingered to have a few words with Fifty.

"Watch what you say to her. Make sure you coach her up on keeping her mouth closed. I know that's yo' girl, but you gotta be careful with this."

"I know," Junior breathed. "That's why I didn't want to put her in it. That shit fucked up."

"What's done is done," Fifty said. "Least you ain't broke no more. I'mma fuck with you later. Love."

"Love," Junior echoed before walking in the house.

Quitta was standing by the door waiting. "What happened? Did y'all kill him?" she asked, her eyes wide with fear and excitement.

Junior didn't answer right away. "I need to take a shower."

Quitta followed him through the house. "Tell me what happened? I'm in this shit too, nigga."

"Be quiet. See if Mama sleep," he said, nodding toward the door as they passed Darlene and Stanley's room.

Quitta mugged him before poking her head inside the room. Stanley, Darlene, and Mooka were all asleep. When she turned to tell Junior, he was gone. She went to the bathroom and found him turning on the water.

"What the fuck happened, Junior? Tell me," she whispered angrily.

"Grab me some clothes," he said, pulling off his shirt.

In the bathroom light, Quitta was able to see dried blood in his hair and a bruise forming on his neck. "Is that blood? Are you okay?" she asked, running her hand through his hair.

"Stop. That ain't my blood."

Quitta looked from the dried blood on her hand and into his eyes. "Is this Fredo's blood?" she asked, her eyes growing wider by the second.

Junior nodded. "Shit didn't go the way we wanted it to go. Nigga tried to take my pistol."

Quitta's eyes grew wider. "What!? How? Wasn't you and Fifty together?"

Junior didn't want to give her too many details, but he also knew she would see it on the news in a couple of days when the police released the gas station footage. "We was supposed to follow the nigga home but when he stopped at the gas station, I tried to get in the truck with him. He jerked the truck, hitting the gas and brakes, and I got slammed into the dashboard. Fat ass nigga dove on me before I could react and started choking me while try'na take the pistol. I thought that nigga had me. I thought he was finna kill me.

42

Fifty seen that something was wrong and blew him down. We left him next to the pumps and burned up both the trucks."

Quitta sat on the toilet looking like she wanted to faint. "Oh my god! I thought y'all was just gon' rob him? So you mean to tell me that y'all killed him and didn't even get nothing?"

"That nigga got his self killed. And we did get something," Junior said, pulling the money from his pockets. "Twenty-five racks."

Quitta looked a little relieved when she saw the money. "Okay. At least we got something. Get in the shower and get that blood off you. I'mma go get some clothes."

While Junior cleaned up, Quitta went to get undressed and grabbed them some pajamas. Then she joined him in the shower. "We can't do that shit no more, baby daddy. What if they trace it back to us?"

"They won't. We good."

"How you know? You know the club got cameras. They gon' see me leave with him."

"But they also gon' see that you wasn't with him at the gas station. If they do come looking for us, we not gon' lie. You gon' say he dropped you off at home, and me and Mama n'em gon' be yo' alibis. When I left the club, I came home. He dropped you off like thirty minutes later. We don't know what happened to that nigga after that. If you stick to the script, we good. But I don't think it's gon' come to that. You wore the wig and makeup. They not gon' be able to identify you. Or me. We good."

Quitta searched his face, wanting something to hold onto and believe in. "I hope you right, baby daddy. I don't want to go back to jail."

"You not going to jail. I promise. Don't even stress yo'self thinking about it. Let's just focus on getting out yo' mama's house. We back! We got money now."

That made Quitta smile. "Thank God. Lord knows I don't ever wanna hear my mama and Stanley's fucking ever again."

"We can move as soon as you find a house," Junior said before leaning forward to kiss her. "Did I tell you how good yo' ass was looking tonight? You was the baddest bitch in that muthafucka."

Quitta's smile got wider. "I was killing it, wasn't I?"

"Hell yeah. You had my dick so hard when we was dancing."

Quitta reached down and began playing with him, watching him grow in her hands. Not wanting his hands to be empty handed, Junior reached between her legs and started rubbing.

"I can't fuck you, baby daddy," she moaned. "I'm still bleeding."

"I know. I'm just doing to you what you doing to me," he said before leaning in for a long tongue kiss.

The lovers moaned and kissed while fondling each other's sex parts. Then Quitta dropped to her knees and began sucking him while the shower sprayed their bodies. Junior gripped the back of her head, pushing more of his dick down her throat, making her gag. Quitta hung in there, keeping eye contact with him while he punished her tonsils. When Junior felt his nut rising, instead of cumming in her mouth like he usually did, he pulled out and sprayed her face. Quitta closed her eyes and fondled his balls until he was empty.

"Damn, yo' ass nasty," Junior moaned, loving the freak in his baby mama.

"I know. That's why you love me," Quitta said while washing her face. When her face was clean, she opened her eyes and saw him watching her and masturbating. "Why you looking at me like that?"

"'Cause I ain't done with you yet. Turn around."

She shook her head. "I told you we can't have sex. I'm still bleeding."

"I know. I wanna fuck you in yo' ass."

Quitta looked surprised. "What?!"

"You heard me. I never did it before and I wanna do it with you. I wanna do everything with you."

Quitta looked unsure. "I think it's gon' hurt, ain't it?"

"I'mma go slow. If it hurt too bad, I'mma stop."

Quitta turned around slowly. "Go slow, Junior," she warned.

When she bent over, he spread her cheeks apart, allowing the water to wet her sphincter. Then he pressed the head of his dick against her asshole and pushed.

"Ah shit!" Quitta yelped, tightening her cheeks. "Stop!"

Junior didn't move. They stayed in that position for almost a minute.

"Okay. Go slow," Quitta said when she was ready.

Junior pushed slowly, listening to Quitta and paying attention to her body. When he was halfway in, he stopped, reaching a hand around her and rubbing her clit.

"Oh, yeah, baby!" Quitta moaned, loving the feeling.

When her body relaxed, he began pumping into her ass slowly, giving her half of him while he rubbed her pearl.

"Damn, Junior. This feel so good!" she moaned, pushing her ass back at him, wanting more.

Junior gave her what she wanted, long stroking her ass while working his fingers. "Yo' ass is so tight, girl. Damn!" he groaned, on the verge of busting again.

"Oh shit, Junior! I'm about to cum, baby! I'm about to cum!"

Junior lifted a hand to cover her mouth while continuing to deliver the pleasure. "Shhh, baby. You getting loud."

Quitta grabbed a hold of his hand that was covering her mouth, pressing it harder against her lips to muffle her moans. She didn't want to make noise, but the pleasure was too intense. Having her ass and clit stimulated at the same time was a new sensation and it was feeling way too good. She could feel her insides bubbling as the orgasm began building. And then it boiled over.

"Oh god!" she screamed before biting down on Junior's hand as her pussy began squirting.

"Ahh, shit!" he groaned, trying to snatch his hand from her mouth.

Quitta had a lock on him like a pit bull, biting harder. She also clenched her ass cheeks, squeezing his dick and forcing him to bust. It took a few moments for her orgasm to pass, and she finally let go of his hand.

"Damn, girl!" he yelled, snatching his stinging hand back and shaking it off.

"I'm sorry, baby," Quitta apologized.

When the stinging finally stopped, Junior examined his hand. Blood dripped from his palm. "Damn, girl! You a muthafuckin' vampire."

"I'm sorry," she apologized again. "Let me see."

Junior allowed her to see his bloody his palm.

"Damn, nigga. You really bit me," he said in disbelief.

Quitta started giggling. "I didn't mean to do that, baby daddy. That shit felt too good and I had to stop myself from screaming before I woke up my mama n'em. I squirted. Did you feel it? I didn't even know I could squirt."

"Hell nah, I didn't feel it. The only thing I could feel was yo' teeth, nigga," he sulked before rinsing his hand under this shower.

***

"Mama, wake up. I'm hungry."

Quitta opened her eyes and saw Mooka's face hovering a few inches away from hers. "Why you all in my face like that?" she asked, pushing him away.

"Because I'm hungry. I want some cake-cakes."

Quitta let out a tired breath. "Okay. Here I come."

Quitta sat up, stretching and yawning before looking toward Junior. He slept peacefully next to her, seemingly unbothered by last night's murder. Quitta, on the other hand, was scared as hell. She wasn't so confident that they would get away Scott free. A man was killed and left in a gas station parking lot. She had seen TV shows like the *First 48* and knew the police would investigate. They were going to trace Fredo's steps back to the club and see her leaving with him. Then it was just a matter of time before they showed up at their door. She wondered if they would come with helicopters and tanks and kick in the door like they did in the movies. She could see her and Junior's faces on Milwaukee's Most Wanted. Prison cells and an ugly fat bitch named Tiny flashed in her head, making her body shiver.

"What the fuck am I doing?" she questioned aloud, shaking the terrifying images from her mind. After getting her mind right, she went to the kitchen to make breakfast. She fixed Mooka's favorite chocolate chip pancakes before making cheese eggs, bacon, and pancakes for her and Junior. After pouring a cup of orange juice, she went to wake and feed her man.

"Junior, wake up!" she called as she walked in the room with the food and drink.

When he didn't move, she sat the plate on the bed and began kissing his neck. "Wake up, baby daddy!" she sang in between kisses.

"Mmmhhh," he moaned, opening his eyes slowly.

"Gmorning, baby daddy!" She smiled.

"Hey. What's up?"

"I made us breakfast," she said, pointing to the plate of food. "Let's eat."

When Junior saw the thick and crispy strips of bacon, he sat up, becoming instantly awake. "Hell yeah, baby mama. You know how to wake a nigga up," he said before sitting the plate on his lap and digging in.

"So, how you plan on getting us out my mama house?" Quitta asked in between bites.

"We gon' use five racks to get the house and fix the truck. Take another five and get us some clothes. I'mma cop with the rest and put us on."

Quitta nodded. "Don't you think we need to put some money up for lawyers and bail?"

Junior was initially thrown by the question. "Where that come from?"

Quitta stopped eating and looked him in the eyes. "They gon' come for us, Junior. I can feel it. We gotta put ourself in a position so that we ready to fight this. We gotta be ready."

Junior acknowledged what she was saying with a nod. "You right, baby. But a couple thousand won't be enough. I'mma run it up and have us ready if they come."

"I also think we need to talk about what comes after hustling. Hustling shouldn't be a forever thing. That was the mistake we made in Lacrosse. We didn't do nothing with the money. We just kept it at home. This time we gotta use the money to buy something that will still be around after the hustle is over. Something that nobody can take from us."

Junior gave Quitta a long look. "I see you been doing a lot of thinking."

"I told you that I know my role. I'm trying to be what you need me to be. I want us to be successful."

"You a boss, baby. And I love yo' boss ass," he said, leaning forward to kiss his woman.

Junior's phone ringing interrupted their make-out session. When he saw the name on the screen, he smiled.

"Who is it?" Quitta asked.

"Six," he told her before answering. "What's up, boss?"

"What's good, nigga? I just got to the city. I'm leaving the airport on the way to Mom's crib. Meet me there."

***

After eating breakfast, Junior got dressed and copped a ride from Darlene to go rent a car. After filling out the paperwork, he pulled off the lot in a 2019 Camaro. His next stop was to find a mechanic to tow the Lexus to a shop to be fixed. After making the arrangements, he drove to his mother's house followed by a tow truck. As soon as he turned onto the block, he spotted Six and a thick brown-skinned woman standing on Doljah's porch. He slowed down and lowered the window.

"I'mma be right back. I gotta take the tow truck to the Lexus," he called before driving down to his mother's house.

After the tow truck driver had the Lexus hitched, Junior walked down to greet his brother and day one, and find out who the woman was.

"Doljah! Six! What it do?" Junior grinned as he approached.

"What's good, my dude?" Doljah smiled.

"What's up, boss? Things must be looking up since you getting the truck towed," Six said as the brothers hugged.

"A real boss will make something out of nothing," Junior quipped.

"Having nothing is just an opportunity for a boss to make something," Six added.

"I just said that," Junior said before turning to Doljah. "Didn't I just say that?"

Doljah laughed and shook his head, recognizing the sibling rivalry. "It was similar, but you didn't say it like Six said it."

Junior blew him off before turning to the woman. She was pretty and thick, flexing her curves in a pair of ripped denim jeans and form-fitting T-shirt. The heels and giant Louis Vuitton glasses added class to the simple style of dress. "What you think? That nigga swagger jacking, ain't he?"

"That's your big brother, so you probably got your swag from him. It ain't jacking if he's the original source."

Six bust out laughing.

Junior looked the woman from head to toe, his mean mug rivaling Ice Cube's famous and hardcore mean mug from the movie *Boyz N the Hood*. "Who is you?"

She took off her glasses and met his stare. "I'm the lady boss. Santana."

Junior looked from Santana to his brother. "This you?"

Six smiled like a boxing coach that watched his trainee throw a knockout blow. "Yeah, nigga. And she trained to go."

Junior cut his eyes back to Santana, giving her a nod of respect. "I like her, brah."

Santana smiled, returning the nod and putting her glasses back on.

"So do I," Six confirmed. "I'm getting a few members of the family together to talk about some major moves. I wanna invite you to the table. You think you ready for the big leagues?"

Junior reacted like he had been slapped. "What kinda question is that? You know I'm ready. I stay ready so I won't have to get ready."

Six let out a chuckle. "That shit sound slick. Let's take a ride. We need to talk. Give Santana the keys."

After showing Doljah some love, the brothers began walking toward Junior's rental when they heard a scream coming from the house next door to their mother's house.

"Do that sound like Nicole?" Six asked.

Before Junior could respond, their baby sister came running out of the neighbor's house. She looked mad, her face twisted up in a mug. Following their sister were three girls that lived next door. One had a small Louisville slugger and another had a knife. "Ayy! What the fuck y'all doing?!" Six yelled, making all the girls stop and look in their direction.

"Nicole!? You good?" Junior called, pulling the pistol from his waist and moving toward his sister. He didn't care if the girls next door were his neighbors. If they attacked his sister, he was going to lay they ass down.

"They try'na jump me, brother, because I beat them hoes' ass!" Nicole bragged, flexing her biceps like a weightlifter. "Look, they got a knife n'shit."

Junior looked at Gina, Tirana, and Ronique. "What the fuck y'all on?"

"That bitch sucka punched me, Junior! I want my get back," Ronique demanded.

"I want mine too," Tirana added.

"Y'all ain't finna jump my sister," Junior said.

"Six, is that y'all sister?" Santana asked, stepping out of her heels and taking off her glasses.

Six smiled like he knew a secret that nobody else knew. "Yeah. That's the baby, Nicole."

Santana walked toward Nicole and nodded. "You need some help, baby girl?"

Nicole nodded. "Hell yeah!"

Santana looked toward the neighbors. "Put that knife and bat down. Let's go. It's three of y'all. What's up?"

The girls looked like they wanted to decline the fight. The bold stranger had them spooked. But they also knew they couldn't duck the action. It was three against two. The odds were in their favor.

"What's up, bitch? You can get it too!" Ronique yelled, dropping the knife and rushing Santana. Tirana dropped the bat and joined her sister in attacking the newcomer. Gina ran at Nicole. Junior and Six watched Santana grab Ronique and throw her to the ground with a perfect hip toss. Tirana tried to tackle Santana from behind, but they ended up tangled in a tussling match. Nicole was exchanging punches with Gina, standing toe to toe like UFC fighters.

"Watch out!" Six called, warning his girl that Ronique was getting up.

Santana moved like she had eyes in the back of her head, kicking a leg out behind her and kicking Ronique in the stomach while still wrestling with Tirana. Ronique stumbled backward and fell on her ass. Knowing that she needed to move quickly, Santana headbutted Tirana, dazing her, before pushing her to the ground. She turned around just in time to dodge a wild swing thrown by Ronique. Then she responded with lefts and rights that she had obviously been practicing on a heavy bag. Ronique didn't stand a chance. She ate the punches like she was at an all you can eat buffet before dropping to the ground. Just as Santana was wrapping up her battle, so was Nicole. She had just landed a punch to Gina's chin that made her stumble.

"I told you I got them hands, bitch!" Nicole bragged when she saw that Gina didn't want no more smoke.

"Damn! They wasn't fucking around!" Junior yelled, excited by the action.

Six gave both of the women high fives. "That's what the fuck I'm talking 'bout. That's how y'all do that shit!"

The front door of their mother's house opened, and Renae stepped outside trying to see what the noise was about. Gina was stumbling up the steps while Tirana was trying to wake up Ronique.

"What the fuck happened?" Renae asked.

"Them hoes tried to jump me and we beat they ass!" Nicole laughed, squatting and shaking her booty toward the losers.

Renae looked toward the neighbors retreating into the house and then Santana. Then she smiled. "Hell yeah, bitch! Damn, why the fuck y'all didn't come and get me?"

"'Cause we had it," Santana said as she slid back into her shoes. "I do this shit for real, baby! Ain't no bitch gon' do nothing to my niggas as long as I'm around. How do my hair look?"

Junior looked toward Six. "She vicious, my nigga. You taught her that?"

Six nodded and smiled. "That's my secret weapon."

Junior gave Santana an approving nod. "Don't let her get away, brah. I like her."

"So do I," Six said, eyeing at Santana like she was an Egyptian Queen.

After taking care of the women next door, Six and Junior hopped in the backseat of the rented Camaro while Santana drove.

"I wanna talk to you about some business, lil' brah. See if you ready to take yo' hustle to the next level," Six said.

"C'mon, my nigga. I already told you I'm ready. Why you keep asking me that?"

The brothers had a long staring contest, neither one of them blinking or smiling. "Because of what happened in Lacrosse. Sounded like you was having yo' way and then you show up in Milwaukee broke. I still don't know how you did that."

"The nigga Steph hit the house while me and Quitta was fucking with you in Vegas."

"Why would you keep yo' money and work where you lay yo' head at? How many times I told you about that shit? What if the police woulda ran in yo' shit instead of that nigga? You would be back up north jacking off to magazines and wondering who Quitta fucking."

Junior mugged his brother, not liking the dig about Quitta. "I know better, my nigga. I know. But the police didn't run in, and a nigga took my shit. Can't cry over spilled milk."

Six nodded. "You right about that. But you can learn how to pour the milk right so you won't spill it. Right?"

Junior nodded. "Yeah."

"So, what you learn from that situation?"

Junior lifted his hands, looking exasperated. "What up with the quiz, my nigga? Is this a test?"

Six gave Junior a dead stare. "You damn right it's a test, nigga. I told you I'm try'na take you to the big leagues. I ain't talking no half a baby and a hundred G's. I'm talking about plugging with a cartel, nigga. TONS of dope! MILLIONS of dollars! And if you ain't ready to carry that kinda weight, I need to know right now because the niggas I fuck with will kill our whole family if you fuck up. So yes, this is a test. And a quiz. And an exam. You hear me?"

Hearing about cartels, tons of dope, and millions of dollars humbled Junior and left him stuck. "Millions?" Junior asked.

Six stared him in the eyes without blinking. "Millions, nigga!"

A quick montage of rich-nigga living ran through Junior's mind. He saw himself partying on yachts, kicking it on a sandy beach in Hawaii, hopping out of a Lamborghini truck. "I'm ready, brah. I never been more ready in my life."

"Tell me about Lacrosse. What you learn?"

Junior thought about the conversation he had with Quitta that morning. "I know that I need to put my money somewhere that no-body can take it. A bank, maybe. I also need to think of what I'mma do after I'm done hustling. This shit ain't supposed to be forever. I'm thinking I need to get involved in real estate. People always need houses. I also learned not to keep my shit where I lay my head at. That shit can get a nigga fucked up."

Six nodded approvingly. "Everything you said was on point. What you learned was how to take an L. That's what all hustlers need to know. You gotta master the art of losing because at some point, everybody gon' take a loss. But you can't let the loss fuck you up. You gotta turn yo' loss into a lesson. That principle can be applied to every aspect of life. When that nigga took yo' shit, he taught you an expensive lesson. Never keep yo' shit where you lay yo' head. And I also like that you thinking about the future. You can't hustle forever. You gotta have an exit plan. I like where yo' head at, Junior. I think you almost ready."

Junior hung onto the word 'almost.' "What you mean 'almost'?"

"It's two things that I need you to do before I put you on the next level. First, I need you to come up with some money. You flat broke?"

Junior smiled, thankful for Fredo's money. "Nah. Me and Fifty made a move last night. I got about twenty."

Six looked surprised. "I see Fif still taking niggas' shit, huh? That's good, but that ain't enough. I need you to turn that twenty into a hundred. That's the fee for a seat at the table."

Junior nodded, going over in his mind all the niggas he could rob to get the money.

"But," Six spoke up, interrupting Junior's thoughts. "You gotta hustle up the money. No more robbing niggas."

Junior gave a helpless look. "C'mon, brah. That's the fastest way to get it."

Six shook his head. "That shit too easy. When you work for something, you appreciate it more. Plus, when you hustle for it, you gon' be able to make some connections that you will need when you touch the new level. Think like a hustler, not a jacker."

Junior shook his head. "Okay. I'mma come up with something. What's the second thing?"

"Parklawn is a gold mine. I had thoughts about taking it over ever since I started hustling, but I didn't have the knowledge or resources to make it happen. When you get your seat at the table, that's gon' be yo' mission. If you can take over the projects, that will be an endless stream of money that you can consistently tap into. That's part two. Come up with a plan to take Parklawn. If you can do those two things, yo' seat at the table will be guaranteed."

Junior thought about the tasks before him. Coming up with 100 G's wasn't that hard. He already did it, so he could do it again. Taking over an entire project seemed impossible. But if he wanted to reach a new level, he would have to do it. "Okay, brah. I'mma do it. I'mma get that money and take over Parklawn. I got it."

Six extended his hand and the brothers shook. "You control yo' own destiny. I didn't think you was ready before, that's why I never let you in on how I've been moving out west. I couldn't bring niggas to the table that wasn't ready because the price was too high. That's why I don't put niggas in my business. I'll give the family whatever they need, but I can't do business with them. Not on this level. Only you and Rocafella. I'm taking him to Arizona and giving him the same opportunity as you."

"What is you doing in Nevada? You fucking with a cartel?" Junior asked, wondering what his brother was involved in.

Six grinned, the secret floating in his eyes. "When the time is right, I'mma tell you everything you need to know. But just know that I fuck with some heavy hitters."

Knowing that Six was fucking with heavy hitters made Junior think about the green light put on him by the Folks. "Aye, brah. Do you think you can help me get the Folks off my ass? Them niggas got a number on my head."

Six gave him a sideways look. "The Folks got a price on ya head? Since when?"

"Since I left Lacrosse. That's the reason we left. I merked a nigga that was plugged and they came at me. Quitta brother said they got a green light on me."

Six got mad. "Why the fuck you just now saying something, nigga? You shoulda told me about this as soon as you found out or at least started the conversation with it. Damn, nigga. This shit serious. You put the whole family in jeopardy. This is the type of shit I was talking about when I was telling you about the big leagues, nigga. This shit serious. Why you off him?"

"Nigga got disrespectful. I let him slide once because I fucked with him. But when he tried to swing on me, I had to get 'em out the way."

Six let out a frustrated breath. He didn't like the situation, but he understood why his brother had to kill. "Okay. Check this out. I'mma talk to my niggas and see if I can get the attention of some heads in Chicago. Until then, don't shoot no more of the Folks, nigga. Can you do that?"

Junior nodded. "I'mma stay low. That's my word."

"I hope yo' word still mean something, nigga. I need you to focus on getting this money. You gotta project to take over. All that other shit don't matter. Focus on the vision."

Chapter 4

After kicking it with Six for the rest of the day, Junior went home to Quitta and his son. They were both in the bedroom. Mooka was playing PlayStation 4 while Quitta had her face in her phone.

"Hey, Daddy! Wanna play the game with me?" Mooka asked.

"Yeah. Let me kick yo' butt, nigga. Gimmie a joystick," Junior said as he sat on the bed next to Quitta.

"Hey, baby mama. What you looking at?"

"I'm looking for stories about Fredo."

That got Junior's attention. "What they saying?"

"The news talked about him earlier and they saying they don't know who did it. But on Facebook they been talking about me. They know he left the club with a female, they just don't know who I am. Yet."

Junior sat the controller down and lay next to Quitta to see her phone. "Let me see."

"Daddy, I thought you was gon' play the game with me," Mooka pouted.

"I'mma catch you later, young money. Me and Mama gotta talk."

Quitta showed Junior the news story and the comments on Facebook. When he looked at her, he saw the fear of prison in her eyes.

"We good, baby. They not gon' find out who you is. You can't worry yourself about this. That's only gon' make it worse."

Quitta's eyes began to water, the tears coming quickly. "I can't help but think about it. I don't want to go to jail. I'm on video with this nigga. Why the fuck y'all have to kill him?"

"C'mon, baby. You know why. The nigga was try'na kill me. What the fuck was we supposed to do? But you gon' be good. They not gon' find out who you is. We good."

Quitta just stared at him. She knew he was trying to comfort her, but it wasn't working. "Is you gon' stay loyal to me if they lock me up?"

Junior frowned. "What kinda question is that?"

"It's a real one. I know it's just a matter of time before they figure out who I am. I'm trying to come to peace with it in my mind. Expect the worst, hope for the best. I just wanna know if you gon' stick by me."

"Listen to me, Quitta. It's not gon' come to that. We good."

Quitta knew better. "I don't care if you fuck some bitches because I know you is. Just don't fall in love or have no bitches around our son. I'll do whatever time they give me. If I gotta take the hit for you to take care of us, I'll do it. I just want you to promise me that you won't fall in love or have no bitches around our son. Do you promise?"

Junior's chest grew warm as he stared in Quitta's tear-stained eyes. She knew in her mind she was going to jail. And deep down inside, Junior knew she was right. She was on video leaving the club with him. Even if she wasn't the actual killer, he knew the courts would treat her like she was. They would pull out all the tactics to get her to snitch. Even sentencing her like she pulled the trigger. "I promise."

Hearing the promise and seeing the truth in Junior's eyes, that they would come for her, made Quitta's tears flow harder. Junior did the only thing he could and wrapped her in a hug.

"What's wrong with my mama?" Mooka asked.

"She sad, man. But I got it."

Mooka dropped the controller and joined his parents in bed, hugging his mother. "Why you sad, Mama?"

"Because I might have to leave in a little while," Quitta cried.

"Why you gotta leave? Where you going?" Mooka asked, on the verge of tears.

"She not going nowhere, young money. She good," Junior said, not wanting their son to worry.

The family continued to lay in bed, comforting one another until Quitta was all cried out.

"Okay. I'm done crying," she said, wiping her eyes. "Light me a cigarette and tell me about your day. Did you figure out how to make some money?"

Junior nodded. "Six want me to take over Parklawn. Said he wanna introduce me to his niggas. It cost a hunnit G's to get a seat at the table. He said we gon' be fucking with cartels and making millions of dollars."

Quitta's eyes grew wide. "Are you serious?! Millions of dollars!?"

"That's what he said. But first I gotta come up with a hunnit G's. And he want me to hustle it up."

Quitta nodded. "I agree. You don't need to be shooting nobody else."

"So, I gotta take this twenty and flip it a couple times. I also gotta figure out how to take over Parklawn. And I gotta do it quick so that we can be ready if them people come at us. We need lawyer money and bail money."

The couple became quiet for a moment. "You gotta build a team, baby daddy. You not gon' be able to do it fast by yourself. You need help."

A light went off in Junior's head. "You right, baby. You exactly right. And I know who to recruit. I'mma get this money and I'mma make sure we straight. That's my word. I'mma make sure we good."

***

"Junior, what's good, my nigga!" Fifty grinned on Facetime.

"Shit ain't looking too good. They talking online about that nigga leaving the club with Quitta. It might only be a matter of time before they connect them dots."

Fifty's smile disappeared. "You want me to knock her out the box? I had to do that to Lisa."

Junior frowned. "Nah, nigga. We ain't finna whack my bitch, fam. She a soljah. If they come, she gon' take her lick."

Fifty didn't look convinced. "You sure? You a be surprised what a cigarette and some McDonald's will get a nigga to say. It's like that shit got some truth serum in them bitch ass burgers. Mu'fucka will tell on his family to get up out them jams. You sure she ready? They always threaten females with they kids. What she gon' do if they threaten to take Mooka?"

"She solid, my nigga. I'm a thousand percent sure."

Fifty shrugged. "Okay. I don't trust her but I trust you. If you believe her, I believe you. But if you wrong, my nigga..."

Fifty didn't finish the sentence. He didn't need to. Junior knew Fifty was going to do whatever necessary to keep his freedom. He would say the same thing if he was in Fifty's shoes.

"We good, my nigga. I just wanted to let you know what was going on."

"Fa sho." Fifty nodded. "I gotta get this shit together for my mama. I'mma shoot through the hood later on and fuck with you."

"A'ight. Love."

"Love."

Junior dropped the phone in his lap and stared out the windshield, replaying the conversation with his childhood friend. The look in Fifty's eyes was serious. Fifty had threatened him without actually saying it. If Junior was wrong about Quitta, if his baby mama got locked up and ran her mouth, he and Fifty would become enemies. That was a scary thought. After pushing thoughts of beefing with his big homie from his mind, Junior climbed from the Camaro and let himself inside the gate at his aunt Lynda's house. He had come to kick it with his cousin, Patricia. She was having a get together. He had also come to holla at his other cousins, T-Murda and RIP, and his little brother, John. They were all going to be a part of his plans to take over Parklawn. He walked around to the backdoor and rang the doorbell.

Patricia answered a few moments later. "Who is it?"

"Junior."

A moment later, the curtain in the door window moved and his cousin's face popped up. Patricia was a dark-skinned woman with shoulder-length hair and had a smile that could light up the night. When the door opened, Patricia greeted him with a smile and a hug. "Hey, cousin!"

"What up, cuz? You look like you feeling good," he commented, noticing her low and red eyes.

"Man, cousin." She smiled, looking high as a kite. "T-Murda got some shit from Afghanistan that is smoking! Come in. Everybody downstairs. I got a surprise for you too."

"What's the surprise?"

She smiled while locking the door. "Come downstairs. You gon' see."

He followed his cousin into the furnished basement where a small party was in full swing. There were about fifteen people downstairs, mostly family. The people that weren't family had been around the family so long that they were like family. They were all chilling, listening to music, smoking, and drinking. Junior walked around greeting everyone.

"Junior, what up, nigga?" T-Murda grinned, showing off his gold-toothed smile. T-Murda was a stocky, dark-skinned nigga that loved dressing up. Today he wore a Balenciaga fit that looked fresh off the rack. When it came to being Dougy, not many people did it better than T-Murda.

"What's good, nigga? Patricia told me you got that Isis pack on deck."

He smiled wide, showing every tooth in his mouth. "On my mama, this shit is a stack for a zip, you hear me? A stack! This shit super stupid."

"Yeah right, nigga!" Junior said in disbelief. "I ain't never heard of no shit costing a stack for a zip."

"That's because you ain't never seen nothing like this," RIP spoke up. RIP was T-Murda's paternal twin brother. He was tall and slim with a neck that looked a little bit longer than average. He was also about that action. RIP had a quick draw like a cowboy in a western movie, and he kept something fat tucked in the waist.

"Where that shit at?" Junior asked, tired of hearing about this super weed. He wanted to see it.

T-Murda dug into the pocket of his Balenciaga coat and pulled out a small jar. "That shit from outer space, cuz."

Junior grabbed the jar and took a better look. There were red, purple, and orangish buds inside with crystals on it.

"What the fuck is this?"

"I told you that shit from outer space, nigga!" T-Murda laughed.

"Let me roll some," Junior said, cracking the jar.

T-Murda grabbed his hand. "You don't disrespect this alien with no papers, my nigga. You put this in a bowl."

"It's like wine tasting, but with weed," Patricia added.

"Who got the bowl?" Junior asked, ready to inhale the super exclusive pack.

John tossed him the weed pipe. "Here you go."

"You don't need that much, my nigga. And hold the smoke in for as long as you can," T-Murda instructed.

"I know how to smoke, nigga." Junior waved him off. "Where my surprise at, Patricia? Is this it?"

"Nah, she upstairs. She should be coming back in a minute."

"She?" Junior asked as he flicked the lighter.

He was about to ignite the weed when the basement door opened. A thick light-skinned woman with green eyes grabbed his attention. The flame disappeared and Junior forgot about the weed as memories of the woman flooded his head.

"Larena!?"

"Hi, Junior." She grinned, showing a perfect smile.

"That nigga seen Larena and said fuck that weed!" John cracked and bust out laughing.

"Fuck you, nigga!" Junior said, waving his little brother off and lighting the weed. He took a big hit. The smoke slid smoothly into his lungs. He removed the bowl from his lips, inhaling again. He tried to hold it, but the smoke seemed like it was on fire. Junior coughed so much that he almost threw up. Everyone in the basement laughed while watching him choke and slob.

Larena brought him a drink and rubbed his back. "Here. Drink this."

When he finally stopped choking, Junior took a sip of the Cîroc, already feeling the potent weed kicking in.

"What the fuck is that!?" he asked when he was finally able to catch his breath. "Why you ain't tell me to take it easy, nigga?"

"That's that alien." T-Murda smiled. "I tried to tell you what it was, but you said you know how to smoke."

"Damn, that shit smoking. Give me the plug. I need some of that."

"You don't think that's too much for you?" Larena giggled.

Junior took another drink, trying to quench the fire in his chest. "That shit might be too much for a regular nigga, but I ain't regular," he responded cockily.

Larena shook her head and laughed. "I see you still a cocky nigga, huh?"

"It ain't cocky if it's the truth, right?"

Larena shook her head again. "I knew you was gon' say that."

The childhood sweethearts shared a long look. Junior remembered everything she was as a teenager and compared it to everything she had become as a grown woman. He remembered her as a cute, light-skinned, thirteen-year-old with big lips and curly hair that came to the middle of her back. That teenager had grown into a woman that was beyond bad. Her hair was still long and curly, piercing green eyes, full lips that looked like they were made to kiss, and a curvy figure that blind niggas would stare at.

"Where you been at?" he asked, unable to stop looking in her eyes.

"I been around. School and working. Had my daughter."

Junior felt a stab when she mentioned having a kid. "How many kids you got?"

"Just one. Like you. How old is your son?"

"Mooka is about to be four. How old is your daughter?"

"She about to be four in September. We had our kids at the same time, huh?"

Junior laughed at the coincidence. He ended up sitting and kicking it with one of his oldest friend for hours, losing track of time. He didn't consider how long he'd been at Patricia's house until his phone rang and Quitta's name showed on the screen. For a moment, he considered not answering but knew that would be bogus considering everything they had been through for the last couple of weeks.

"I'mma be right back," he told Larena before stepping into the hallway and answering the phone. "Hey, baby mama."

"Hey, baby. Where you at?"

"Over at Mom's house. What's going on?"

"Come outside. I'm with my mama and we finna pull up."

Junior's eyes grew wide and he panicked a little bit as he realized he was about to be caught in a lie. "Um, I'm busy right now. What you need?"

"You busy?" Quitta questioned. "What that got to do with you coming outside?"

Knowing he was busted, Junior did what all guilty people did and got mad. "Why the fuck you interrogating me? What you want?"

"I'm not interrogating you, nigga. What the fuck wrong with you? I came to talk to you about the house me and my mama just came from seeing. Bring yo' ass outside because we pulling up right now."

Junior tried to think of another lie, but nothing came to mind. Plus, Quitta was already at his mother's house. Once she went inside, he would be busted. "I just told you I'm busy. I'mma meet you at yo' mama house."

"Oh, hell nah, Junior. Bring yo' ass outside. Matter of fact, I'm on my way in the house. Where you at?"

Junior shook his head, thinking of another lie. "I ain't in the house. I'm in Parklawn. But I'm busy. I'mma meet you at the crib."

Quitta got mad. "Where the fuck is you at, Junior? Why you lying? You by a bitch house?"

"Nah, I ain't by no bitch house. I said I'm busy. I'm try'na get a plug. I'mma meet you at yo' mama house."

"Tell me where you at right now, Junior! I ain't playing, nigga."

"Man, I just told you I'm busy. I'mma see you when I get home. Bye."

He hung up the phone and leaned against the wall, staring at the ceiling. He got caught in a lie and when he got home, he would have to argue with Quitta. Something he didn't feel like doing. When the phone rang again, he checked the screen. It was Quitta. When he didn't answer, she began texting. He let out a chuckle before dropping the phone in his pocket and going back into the basement.

Larena watched him, reading his body language as he sat next to her.

"You good?"

He chuckled and let out a stressed breath. "Yeah."

"That was yo' baby mama, huh?" she asked, already knowing.

"Yeah," Junior answered truthfully. "And I just got caught in a lie. I told her I was at Mom's crib and she was right out front."

Larena laughed. "That's messed up. Why you lie to her?"

"'Cause I didn't want her to come over here."

"You should've let her come. We ain't doing nothing wrong."

"Too late for all of that now. I'm finna holla at cuzzo n'em and then get out of here. Let me get your number before I go."

Larena smiled. "You sure that's a good idea? I'm not try'na mess up a happy home."

"You let me worry about my happy home, okay?"

After getting Larena's number, he gathered John, T-Murda, and RIP in the bedroom. "Aye, I wanna holla at y'all about a play," Junior began. "Six want me to take over Parklawn. I think the best way to do that is build a team. Y'all my niggas and family, so I wanna know if y'all wanna fuck with me."

"Take over Parklawn?" T-Murda frowned.

"How four niggas gon' take over a whole project?" John asked.

"The best way we know how. Six offered me a seat at the table with niggas that's making millions. Cartels n'shit. But I gotta bring him a hunnit first. That's how much it cost to get a seat at the table."

"Millions of dollars?" RIP asked skeptically.

Junior shook his head. "Millions."

"Six plugged in with cartels?" T-Murda asked.

"He wouldn't say all that, but I think he is. That's why him and Polo went out west to get money. Now they try'na put the family on. This our opportunity to get some real money. Do some shit that niggas never dreamed of. So, what y'all wanna do? Y'all wanna do this shit or what?"

"You still ain't said how we gon' take over a whole project," John said. "It's plenty of niggas hustling out there. What, we just supposed to take over them niggas' shit?"

"Not right away, but eventually. First we gotta come up with a hunnit G's so I can plug in. I see it like this. If we plug with a cartel, we gon' have the best product. Best dope. Best weed. Best pills. And we gon' have a lot. We can supply everybody. Low numbers to start off so niggas eat it up. Before we know it, we got everybody buying everything from us."

The cousins all got lost in thought, dollar signs floating through their heads.

"Damn, Junior. I think you might be on to something. I'm in." John smiled.

Junior looked toward the twins. "What y'all wanna do?"

"Shit, you had me at millions," RIP said. "I'll kill every nigga in Parklawn for that. I'm in."

"I'm in too," T-Murda spoke up. "But we gotta talk about this hunnit. How much you got already?"

"I got twenty. What y'all got?"

"I got like five," T-Murda said.

"I got the same," RIP said.

John didn't say anything.

"What you got, nigga?" Junior asked.

"Man, brah. Shit tight."

Junior lifted his hands. "What the fuck that mean?"

"I got like fifteen hunnit."

Everyone laughed.

"How you talk all that money shit and only got fifteen hunnit?" RIP asked.

"Because I'm rich in spirit, nigga," John shot back.

"Aight. This what we gon' do. I'm finna holla at S'n'Lo and see if we can catch a half a brick. Then we gon' turn that bitch until we get the hunnit."

"Make sure that shit valid," T-Murda spoke up. "You know niggas out here with that bullshit because of this COVID shit."

"You know I already know. I'mma make sure we good. Just make sure y'all stack. The faster we get the hunnit, the faster we make the plug. Let's holla at cuz n'em a little longer, and then I'mma need y'all to grab that paper so I can get up with S'n'Lo."

After establishing their next move, the cousins went back to the party. A couple minutes later, the doorbell rang. Patricia went to answer and came back downstairs with Lo-Dog. He walked in the basement smiling, showing love to the family. As soon as Junior saw him, he knew it was time to leave.

"Aye, y'all. I'mma get up outta here."

"Junior, what you on, cuz?" Lo-Dog asked.

"I ain't on shit," Junior mugged, heading toward the door.

"We still on that? For real?"

Junior looked him right in the face, hostility showing in his eyes. "Yeah, we still on that. For real."

"C'mon, cuz. I ain't finna keep apologizing. How you gon' fuck with Quitta but still be on that with me? That ain't no real nigga shit."

Junior looked him up and down. "Don't talk to me about no real nigga shit, 'cause you definitely ain't no real nigga. You a snake, fam, and I don't wanna be around no snakes. Gotta keep the grass cut and stay away from niggas like you," he said before turning to his new teamsters. "I need y'all to grab that paper so I can make that move."

John and the twins said a few words to everyone in the basement before leaving. Once they were outside, Junior made the call to S'n'Lo. "What up, nigga? Where you at?"

"I'm over here at Uncle Joe's getting fitted. What up?"

"I need to holla at you about a move. Stay where you at. I'm on my way."

When Junior got to Uncle Joe's, he found S'n'Lo inside with a team of hustlers. Ricky Blow, Moon, and Cheese were trying on clothes and shoes.

"I see y'all niggas try'na buy the whole store," Junior laughed, greeting the Parklawn hustlers.

"I gotta do a show tonight in Madison. Y'all niggas should come," Ricky Blow said while checking his Fendi fit in the mirror.

"Madison?" Junior questioned.

"On the low, Madison coming up on that rap shit," Cheese chimed in.

"I'm just going to grab me something new to jump up and down on," Moon said. "Madison got them professional hoes. I need one or two of them in my life."

"Ain't nothing wrong with that," Junior said before turning to S'n'Lo. "What's good, Lo? Come holla at yo' boy."

"Aye, don't touch my Giuseppes," S'n'Lo warned his niggas before walking away with Junior. "I got the last pair of green and black ones and I know Moon wanted 'em. But what's up with you, Junior?"

"I need some work. Like a half a book."

S'n'Lo stopped in an empty isle and gave Junior a suspicious look. "You want a half a book?"

"Yeah, nigga. I'm try'na eat."

"I thought you be taking niggas' shit. What you on?"

Junior laughed. "C'mon, Lo. I wouldn't do you like that. You my nigga. I'm really try'na hustle. I can't keep stripping niggas. That shit starting to get dangerous. I'm ready to hustle full time. What that half a book gon' run me?"

S'n'Lo gave him a long look. "I can probably get it for twenty-five. Prices up because of this bitch ass coronavirus."

Junior nodded. "I been hearing the same shit. Put me an order in. Make sure it ain't no bullshit. I'm finna go grab the money. How long 'til you ready?"

"I'mma call my nigga Wood right now and then let you know. But, before I do that, I need to holla at you about something," he said, his demeanor becoming a little more serious.

"What's good?" Junior asked, noticing the change in his demeanor.

"Was that you that hit Fredo?"

Junior wasn't expecting the question and couldn't contain his surprise. "What? What the fuck you talking about?"

S'n'Lo continued to stare at him, looking for a tell-tale sign. "Fredo got killed after leaving the club last weekend. His niggas got a picture of a bitch that look like yo' baby mama. Was that you?"

Junior couldn't hide the distress. Hearing the niggas were float-ing around a picture of his baby mama fucked with him. "What they saying? Do they know who she is?"

An "I knew it look" showed in S'n'Lo's eyes. "Damn, nigga. Yo' ass hot as fuck, nigga!"

Junior didn't want to hear that shit. "Fuck that bitch ass nigga. What they saying? Do they know who she is?"

S'n'Lo shook his head. "Nah. The picture wasn't that good. It was mainly of her ass, but you can see her face a little bit. Only reason I knew it was her is because I seen her so much. That pink hair was making me second guess, though."

Junior closed his eyes and let out a frustrated breath. "Damn. These bitch ass niggas got a picture, huh?"

S'n'Lo nodded.

"Tell me about these niggas. They got shooters or is they bud-dies with the police?"

"A lil' bit of both. They the kinda niggas that will pistol play a little bit, but if shit get too serious, they might call them people." Junior took a moment to think about what he was told. He was in a fucked-up spot. They had a picture of his girl, and if he hit them niggas too hard, they would call the police. He was stuck between a rock and a dope fiend.

"A'ight, Lo. Good looking on the heads up. Don't say nothing about this to nobody. Not even yo' niggas."

S'n'Lo nodded. "I know how it go. You good. I'mma call Wood and get that work for you."

Junior left the store with a lot on his mind. They had a picture of Quitta. He wanted to call his niggas and bend on Fredo's niggas, but knowing they might be the type to call the police if shit got too heavy made him hesitate. If the police got their hands on the picture, it would only be a matter of time before they came knocking. The last thing he wanted to do was make a bad situation worse. He needed more time to figure out what to do. Text messages from T-Murda and RIP took his mind off the fucked-up predicament for a moment. They had their money and wanted to know where to meet. He texted them to meet him in the hood. The next text came from

S'n'Lo. His guy was ready. Junior texted back that he was getting ready and would call in ten minutes. When he pulled up to the house, he dashed inside to get the money. Quitta was waiting for him in the living room. The hostility on her face told of her mood. She was ready for a fight.

"Where the fuck you was at, nigga!?"

He walked past her, heading for the bedroom. "I don't got time for that shit right now."

Quitta chased him. "What the fuck you mean you don't got time? Nigga, you better make time. Why the fuck you lie to me? Where was you at, Junior?"

He ignored her, going into the drawer to get the money.

"Hello! You hear me talking to you, nigga!?" Quitta yelled, getting in his face.

"Move, nigga!" he yelled, pushing her away. "Get the fuck out my face!"

Quitta reacted like he punched her. "Don't be putting yo' fucking hands on me, bitch ass nigga!" she yelled before shoving him back.

Junior stumbled backward into the dresser. For the briefest moment he considered beating Quitta's ass. He was already stressed about Fredo's niggas having her picture and didn't feel like arguing about his petty lie. "You better watch yo' fucking mouth, nigga!" he warned.

Quitta knew that Junior wasn't going to hit her. Not while her mother and Mooka were in the other room. "Or what, nigga? Fuck you gon' do?" she yelled, getting in his face. "Why the fuck you lie to me? Tell me where you was at? You got another bitch? Was that who you was with?"

Junior's top lip began twitching as his face twisted into a mug. He wanted to punish Quitta for her actions. She was really testing him. But instead of beating her ass, he decided to humble her with the news about her picture. "You wanna know where I was at, nigga? Huh? You really wanna know?"

Quitta continued to stare at him defiantly. "Yeah, nigga. Be a man. Tell me where you was at."

"I was with my nigga S'n'Lo try'na save yo' stupid ass. Fredo niggas been showing yo' picture to niggas try'na find out who the fuck you is. That's where the fuck I been. Try'na save yo' ungrateful ass."

The news made Quitta back down a little bit, the anger in her eyes changing to fear. "You for real, Junior? Don't be lying and try'na change the subject because I caught yo' ass in a lie."

"Why the fuck would I play about something this serious? I wasn't with no bitches. I was try'na get my hands on that picture, and I didn't wanna tell you what I was doing because I didn't want you to worry. I was try'na fix it. Yeah, I lied, but not because I was with a bitch."

Quitta backed away from him and sat on the bed, her life and freedom flashing before her eyes. "Oh my god! Oh my god!" she repeated, her tears flowing like a rushing river. "They got my picture. I'mma go to jail. I can't believe this shit. Oh my god!"

Junior tucked the money in his pocket before sitting next to Quitta on the bed. "I'mma figure this out, Quitta. For real. I got you. But, just to buy time, hurry up and get the house so you can have somewhere to lay low at. You said something about a house earlier. What was you talking about?"

"I don't even remember right now. I can't stop thinking about the picture. Oh my god! What about our son? What am I gon' do?"

"Quitta, I need you to chill. We gotta think. You panicking ain't gon' change shit. Stay with me. What did they say about the house?"

"Oh my god. Okay. Okay. I'mma calm down. Okay," she repeated, taking deep breaths. "They said we can move in as soon as we ready. They was holding it for somebody, but something happened and the other people didn't sign the lease. That's what I wanted to talk to you about to see when you wanted to move in. I could've signed it earlier."

"Okay. Call them back and see if we can sign the lease tonight then we can move in tomorrow. Can you do that?"

Quitta nodded, wiping tears from her face. "Yeah. I can," she whined. "Baby, I'm scared. I don't want to go to jail."

Junior wrapped her in a hug. "I told you that I got you, baby. I'mma try to fix it. I got yo' back. We a team, remember? Us against the world."

Chapter 5

One month later

"Daddy, wake up. Wake up, Daddy!"

Junior opened his eyes to Mooka's face inches away from his. "What's up, man?"

"Mama want you."

"What?" Junior asked, confused about why Mooka was waking him up for Quitta. "What she want?"

"I don't know. Mama told me to wake you up. She want you."

Junior let out a grunt before rolling over. "If she want something, tell her to come to me."

Mooka jumped off the bed and ran from the room. "Mama, Daddy said if you want something come to him!"

Junior and Quitta's relationship had become rocky. All they did was argue as of late, and all the signs pointed to their relationship coming to an end. Nothing he did was right and everything she did wasn't good enough. Every time he came home late, which was almost every night, she accused him of being with another woman. His excuse was the hustle. He was really trying to get that hundred G's so he could get a seat at the table with cartel bosses. They would need the money for lawyers and bail. And that took being on the grind constantly. Quitta didn't understand that. She was used to the way he hustled in Lacrosse. She went with him on most of the serves and he was normally at home by ten or eleven o'clock. No later than midnight. But the hustle in Milwaukee was different. He had to be available at all hours. Junior had just gotten comfortable when he heard Quitta's feet shuffling into the room.

"Why you couldn't get up to see what I wanted?"

Junior kept his eyes closed and his back to her. "Because I was sleep. If you wanted something, you should've came to me."

"You don't tell yo' niggas or them bitches to wait. Every time yo' phone ring yo' ass go running up outta here, but if I want something, it's a problem."

"When my phone ring, it's about some money. How you think the bills and all that shit get taken care of? How you think we gon' be able to afford lawyers and bail money? They showing yo' picture on the news as a person of interest. I gotta put shit together for when they come."

"I don't know who the fuck you think I am. Nigga, I ain't stupid. I know you out there fucking bitches. That's why yo' ass don't come home 'til one or two o'clock in the morning. That's why you don't want me to come with you. Let me catch yo' ass, and I swear to God I'mma fuck you up."

"Man, shut the fuck up, nigga. All you do is complain and talk shit. That's why I stay out late 'cause I don't wanna hear all that bitch ass shit you talking about. Leave me the fuck alone," he snapped while fluffing his pillow and trying to get comfortable.

Quitta walked around to the other side of the bed so she could see his face. "Nah, nigga. You stay out late because you fucking off. Being a hoe with all yo' hoe friends. Why you didn't stay out this late in Lacrosse? Yo' ass was in the house with me every night. Now I gotta beg yo' ass to come home. What the fuck changed, Junior? What the fuck changed?"

Junior sat up, his face twisted up in frustration. "How many times I gotta tell you this shit, Quitta? Selling dog food is different than crack. Them white muthafuckas in Lacrosse get a couple grams and they be good for a lil' minute. Muthafuckas that smoke woo need that shit twenty-four-seven. I'm not out there cheating and being a hoe. I'm try'na get a seat at the muthafuckin' table so I can get this money. That's it. We gon' need bail money and lawyer money too. I'm try'na put us in the best position to be able to fight this if they identify you. What the fuck don't you understand about that?"

"Then why you don't wanna fuck me no more? You don't tell me I'm pretty or you love me. Nothing."

"You the one that don't wanna fuck. Every time I tried, you told me not to touch you."

Quitta looked thoughtful for a moment. "That's because I know you fucking somebody else. A woman's intuition don't lie."

Junior shook his head while waving a hand, blowing her off. "You can believe whatever the fuck you wanna believe. I ain't finna keep explaining myself."

"Why don't you just leave me, Junior? Why? Because I know you want to. You wanna go fuck all yo' little Parklawn thots. The only reason you probably staying is because you think I'mma snitch on you when the police find out who I am."

"Who the fuck said anything about me leaving? I ain't going nowhere. I told you I'mma ride this out."

"That's what yo' mouth say, but yo' actions say something different. If you wanna leave, why you don't just leave?"

"Man, I don't got time for this bullshit," Junior said before getting out of bed and grabbing his clothes.

"That's right. Do like you always do and run to yo' mama house with all yo' little Parklawn bitches. I hope one of them bitches give you herpes or AIDS, nigga."

When Junior was in the Lexus truck, he sat in the driveway trying to gather himself and figure out what the fuck was going on in his life and relationship. He lived in a two-bedroom house in Wauwatosa, a suburb on the outskirts of Milwaukee, where the police and crime was almost nonexistent. The house was furnished with the best of everything. Big screen TVs, video games, new appliances. Mooka and Quitta had everything they wanted and needed. He thought things would get better when he started getting money again and was able to take care of the family. But that wasn't true. If anything, shit had gotten worse.

It was so bad that some nights he thought about not even coming home. He wanted to remain loyal to Quitta and help her through the legal troubles that were surely about to come her way. The last thing he wanted to do was leave her fucked up, especially since Fredo's niggas had her picture and the police had given the footage from inside the club to the media and it was being shown on the news. But it seemed like Quitta was trying to push him away. He couldn't figure out how they had gon' from ride or die to enemies. Everything he did was for her and Mooka. He bussed his ass and took risks in the streets to get them to another level. To make it so if the police ever did kick in their door, they would have enough to be represented by the best lawyers. But Quitta didn't believe his intentions and he couldn't understand why. Shit didn't make sense.

After trying and failing to rationalize his situation, he left home for the stash house. He learned his lesson from Lacrosse and no longer kept the work where he lay his head. Instead, he rented an efficiency apartment for $500 a month. This was where he kept the work and he was the only one with a key. He loved his cousins and little brother, but he wasn't giving them access to the apartment. He would be responsible for safe keeping the drugs. He liked the location of the apartment because it was in a good neighborhood where people paid attention to who belonged and who didn't, and you needed a key to get inside the eight-unit apartment building. As far as he was concerned, the apartment was a safe space. Nobody knew where it was and nobody was allowed inside but him.

He parked in the back of the building and used the key to unlock the door before taking the flight of stairs to his apartment. The apartment was barely furnished with a two-piece couch and sofa, a TV, and a stove in the kitchen for cooking the dope. Once inside, he went to the kitchen cabinet and pulled out three baggies half filled with rocks. Each bag held one ounce of crack broken down into 200 rocks, each rock worth fifteen dollars apiece. That made each bag worth 3,000 dollars. Since the world was in the middle of a pandemic, drug prices skyrocketed and addicts complained about being ripped off or being sold bad product. Junior's plan was to sell fifteen-dollar bags of good dope.

T-Murda, RIP, and John thought the plan was crazy until the money started rolling in. In a month they had made over 150,000 dollars. Junior stashed the money at home and was waiting on Six to come in town so he could take the money and get him a seat at the table. After pocketing one of the 3,000-dollar sacks, he locked the door and went to get something to eat before heading to the hood. It was a couple minutes after nine o'clock in the morning when he drove past the "Welcome to Parklawn Housing Project" sign and turned onto 47th and Congress. He immediately noticed two black and white patrol cars and a blue unmarked sedan outside his mother's house. Instead of stopping, he drove by, trying to see if they were inside his mother's house. The cars were empty and the front door was closed, so he couldn't see inside.

"What the fuck!?" he cursed as gloomy thoughts of jail cells flashed in his head.

Had the police found out who Quitta was? Did they identify him too? Was it time to go on the run?

"Chill, Junior," he told himself, trying not to wig the fuck out.

He drove to the next block, parking in front of Toe Tagga's house and calling his mother to figure out why the hell the police were parked outside.

"They just came and took your sister to jail," Gail cried.

"What? Who? What happened?" Junior asked, his voice high pitched and cracking.

"Nicole. They said she robbed somebody and Q got shot."

Junior couldn't believe his ears. "Who shot Q? Who Nicole rob?"

"Junior, I can't talk right now. I'm still try'na figure it out myself. Come home. I gotta go."

Click.

Junior stared out the windshield for a moment, confused by everything he heard. Q was his godbrother that he hadn't seen in forever. How in the fuck did his baby sister get caught up in a robbery with Q? When he realized the police weren't there for him or Quitta, he jumped from the Lexus, leaving the work inside, and ran toward his mother's house. He walked through the door and saw his mother and Renae sitting on the couch. A tall dark-skinned man with a thick mustache wearing a blue suit and two police officers stood in front of them.

"What happened?" Junior asked his mother.

"They saying Nicole and Q robbed a policeman and he shot Q," Gail cried.

"Who are you?" the detective asked, giving Junior a head-to-toe look.

Junior returned the look. "Who is you?"

"I'm Detective Johnson. And you are?"

Junior wasn't about to tell the police his name. They might use it to connect him to something later. Like Fredo's body. "Why you asking my name? You not here to talk to me."

"Bro, chill," Renae spoke up, sensing the tension between the cop and her brother.

Detective Johnson gave Junior a long look before turning back to Gail. "We need you to come down to the station so we can question your daughter. She's a minor and we can't talk to her without a parent or guardian."

"Okay. I just need to grab my purse," Gail said as she walked to her room. "I'll be right back."

Junior followed his mother to the room. "Make sure she don't talk without a lawyer, Mama. She don't gotta answer they questions."

"Boy, she about to be in trouble for robbery. I ain't finna let my baby get caught up in this bullshit. I know what to do."

"Just make sure she got a lawyer there before she answer any questions."

"I know. I went through this with you. I got it."

After grabbing her purse, Gail left with the police. Detective Johnson gave Junior a smirk on his way out the door.

"How the fuck Nicole end up robbing somebody with Q?" Junior asked Renae.

"Shit, I don't know. She told Mama she was going by her friend Jennifer's house last night. Then we got woke up with these muthafuckas banging on the door asking questions."

Junior shook his head. "Man, this shit crazy as fuck. What the fuck was that nigga Q on?"

"On some bullshit. Him and Nicole must've been setting niggas up. They said she got the off-duty police attention and Q tried to come from behind and rob him, but the police saw him coming. Shot him in the chest and almost killed his ass."

Junior just shook his head, trying to figure out when his little sister had gone from liking Hello Kitty and cartoons to setting niggas up to get robbed. "Man, I don't even know what to say, sis. This a wild ass morning," Junior said before flopping down on the couch.

"Who you telling! This the last shit I expected to wake up to. Why you up so early?"

Junior let out a stressed breath. "Quitta muthafuckin' ass wanna argue about dumb ass shit early in the morning."

Renae laughed. "What was it today?"

He shrugged. "Man, I don't even know. She had Mooka wake me up and when I didn't go see what she wanted, we started arguing. I just left."

"It's probably the case hanging over her head that's making her stressed out, and she taking it out on you. If they was looking for yo' ass for a murder, you'd probably be pissed off at anything and everything too."

Junior thought about his sister's words. "That kinda makes sense. But I still don't wanna hear that bullshit every time I come in the house. That shit make me not wanna go back home."

"You a be a'ight, brother. You know what you need?"

"Some loud," Junior chuckled.

Renae lifted her eyebrows. "You just read my mind."

While getting high with his sister, Junior called Six.

"What's up, boss?" Six answered, sounding half asleep.

"Man, brah. I don't even know how to tell you this shit," Junior mumbled.

Six became instantly alert. "What's up, boss? Something happen to Mama? What's good?"

"Man, Nicole in jail for robbery."

"Nicole in jail for robbery?" Six asked, not believing what he heard.

"Yeah. Mama just left with the detective to be there when they question her."

Six raised his voice. "How the fuck Nicole get locked up for robbery, nigga? Who the fuck she rob?"

"She was with Q. They tried to set up an off-duty police officer, and he shot Q."

"Oh my god, boss! Are you serious?"

"Yeah," Junior breathed. "I just found out."

"How the fuck she end up with Q? Where the fuck was you?"

"I was at home. She told Mama she was gon' be by her friend's house but ended up with Q."

Six let out a heavy breath. "Man, I can't believe this shit. What the fuck, Junior? I told you to watch over the family, nigga. I told you to make sure everybody was good and taken care of."

"Man, I can't be with everybody at all times. She seventeen years old. I can't hold her hand."

"It ain't about holding her hand. It's about letting her know her place in the world. Her role as a young woman. Man... Never mind. I'mma be in the city tomorrow. I'mma holla at you when I get in town."

Click.

"What he say?" Renae asked.

Junior shook his head. "That nigga making it seem like it's my fault. I can't hold her hand. She damn near grown."

"You can't tell him that. He think we all still kids."

Junior sat for a moment, brooding over the conversation with his older brother. He didn't know what more he could've done for Nicole. Plus, nobody could change what happened. Nicole was going to have to fight the case with a lawyer. All he could do was help out when she needed. After finishing the blunt with Renae, his phone started ringing, so he hit the block to hustle. He made a few serves before making his way to Jeff's spot. Jeff was an older, chubby, bald-headed nigga that used to have money before he started smoking his own supply. Now he was one of Junior's best customers, and he let Junior and his niggas make plays out his Parklawn apartment for a couple bags a day.

"Junior! What's going on, baby boy!" The cluck smiled, happy to see his favorite drug dealer.

"What's good, Jeff? How you living?" Junior asked as he stepped into the sparsely furnished apartment.

The living room consisted of a couple of cheap blue suede couches, a table with a PlayStation 4 and games atop, and a 40-inch TV on the wall.

"Shit, I'm good now that you here. You know a nigga need that wake up. You still got that A-1?"

Junior pulled the fat sack from his pocket and dropped two rocks in Jeff's open palm. "That right there gon' give yo' chest hairs a perm every time you take a hit."

"That's that shit I'm talking 'bout!" Jeff smiled. "I'mma go get myself together and then go outside and bring 'em in. You know how we do. Every five and I get mine."

"I wouldn't have it no other way," Junior said, cutting on the TV and grabbing a PlayStation 4 controller. Junior sat, smoking weed and making serves while playing Madden. John showed up later, followed by T-Murda and RIP. He filled them in on what happened to Nicole before the conversation turned to money.

"When is that nigga Six gon' get you a seat at the table?" T-Murda asked.

"On the gang. Niggas ready to eat big boy plates," RIP added.

"He supposed to be here tomorrow. Now that Nicole in a jam, I think he gon' be here for sure," Junior answered.

"When you get to the table, you gotta see if you can get a plug for everything," John spoke up. "If we wanna lock up the whole projects, we need pills, loud, dog food, and that white."

"I been thinking about that same shit." Junior nodded. "If these niggas is who Six say they is, then I think they gotta have it all. Then we can each have our own building moving our shit. I'mma fuck with that white girl and hard. What y'all want?"

"I want the pills. See if you can get it all. Perc, molly, X, zans. All that shit," T-Murda said.

"I want that Great Dane," RIP said. "I gotta couple old heads that I can get back on line. Most niggas got fentanyl on they shit. I know some pops that want real uncut food."

"I guess I'mma move that loud pack," John said. "Y'all niggas don't know what y'all missing. The weed man get all the pussy."

"That's 'cause we ain't thinking about pussy, nigga. We thinking about paper, nigga," RIP laughed.

"You don't know what you talking about," T-Murda jumped in. "The nigga with the beaners get all the hoes. I know some bitches that a go crazy for a 30."

While his niggas were going back and forth about who was going to sell what, Junior got a call that made him tune his niggas out.

"Larena, what's good?"

"Hey, Junior. Um, are you busy right now?" she asked, her voice a little stressed.

"Nah. I'm posted. What's good?"

"Man, my stupid ass car won't start and I need to get to my daughter's daycare. Can you help me out?"

Junior dropped the game controller and stood. "Fa sho. I got you. Where you at?"

"I'm at work. Do you know where the Harper House Group Home is on Riverside?"

"Nah. But I'll find it. Gimmie like twenty minutes."

"Okay. Thanks, man. I appreciate it."

"For sure." After hanging up the phone, Junior turned to his niggas. "I gotta make a move. Holla if you need me."

"Larena, huh?" John grinned.

"Find you some business, lil' nigga."

With a little help from GPS, Junior was able to find the group home. It was a big purple house with a gate surrounding it on Milwaukee's upper east side. After parking, he called Larena to let her know he was outside. She stepped onto the porch a few moments later looking like a twenty piece. She wore her hair in a natural curly ponytail, light makeup on her face with red lipstick, a white Fendi T-shirt, ripped Fendi jeans, and heels.

"Thanks for coming to get me," she said, smelling like everything good as she hopped in the passenger seat of the Lexus.

"You know I got you. What's that perfume you wearing? Shit smell like heaven."

"Thank you. It's Chanel. I like the way it smells too. It's my favorite perfume."

"It's my favorite, too," Junior cracked.

"You silly," she laughed.

"Where the daycare at?"

"It's over on 70th and Villard. It's my cousin's. I just need to pick up a prescription from Walgreens for my daughter's ear infection and drop it off. She been acting a fool with this earache."

"Them ear infections ain't no joke. When Mooka had his, he was on some Tasmanian devil shit. Nigga was screaming from sun up to sun down."

"That's exactly how Kamari is. She be doing the most. Had me up at four o'clock this morning. I'm tired as hell," she yawned. After picking up the prescription, they headed to the daycare to drop off the medicine and then back to the group home. During the ride, Junior's phone rang constantly. A couple of the calls and texts were from Quitta but most were action. Junior didn't answer any of the calls because he didn't want anything to interrupt his time with Larena.

"You not gon' answer the phone?" Larena asked.

"They can call back later. Right now I'm vibing with you."

"What about your girl?" Larena fished.

"Oh, we finna go there, huh?" Junior chuckled. "What about her?"

"Was that her calling?"

"Yeah. She called a couple of times. But it was mostly action."

"You could've answered. I wasn't gon' say nothing or start acting funny."

Junior nodded. "Okay."

The car became quiet for a moment. "Did she really fuck Lo-Dog?"

He laughed. "Who told you about that?"

"Lo-Dog said something about it after you left Patricia's house. He was mad that you forgave her but not him."

"Yeah. That really happened. And the reason I forgave her and not him was because I feel like he betrayed me more. That was my nigga. Everything I learned about the streets came from him. He was one of the main niggas I asked for advice besides my brother. I didn't think he would do me like that."

"I get it. But how could you stay with her after she fucked your cousin?"

"She did it to get back at me for fucking her sister-in-law. We both crossed them lines that shouldn't be crossed, you know what I'm saying? What she did was bogus as fuck. No doubt. But I kinda started that shit. Plus we just had a miscarriage, and we already got Mooka and we wanna raise him with two parents. And she probably finna have to take a case for me."

Larena nodded. "I understand that. I felt the same way with Kamari's daddy. I forgave that nigga for a lot of shit because I wanted our daughter to have both parents. But that nigga thought I was gon' keep forgiving him and he kept on cheating on me. Then one day I finally got fed up and kicked his ass out. Now he don't even wanna help take care of our daughter because I don't wanna be with him. Sometimes I ask myself what I ever seen in that nigga and why I let him get me pregnant. What kinda man won't take care of his daughter because he can't be with her mother?"

"A nigga that's not a man. I think we too quick to call a nigga a man just because they turn eighteen or start having kids. That's not what makes a man. Alotta niggas think they a man because they get pussy, got some money, had some kids, or shot some niggas. But that ain't it. You can tell a man by the choices he makes. By his priorities. By the way he shows love and takes care of the people that depend on him. A man ain't gon' run out on his responsibility."

Larena nodded. "Damn, Junior. That makes so much sense. All these niggas ain't men. You right. We too quick to give them a title they don't deserve. The same thing goes for a woman, you know? Just because she had your son don't mean she's a woman. A lot of people think a woman's power is her pussy. But a real woman's power is between her ears, not her legs."

"Talk that shit to me, baby!" Junior said, lifting his hand for a high five.

The teenage sweethearts shared a look that said more than any words they could speak. Desire, passion, and a litany of what ifs showed in their eyes.

"I wonder what would've happened if we hadn't lost contact," Larena thought out loud. "I wish you were my daughter's father. I think both of our lives would've been way different."

Junior thought about her words. "I think life happens the way it's supposed to. Mistakes gotta happen. That's how we learn and grow. Plus, bad times make you appreciate good times more. That's that whole thing about appreciating the summer after going through winter. We appreciate these moments with each other because of everything that we been through."

Larena nodded, looking at Junior through a new set of eyes. She had always been attracted to him since they were kids, but now the attraction was deeper. Not only was she attracted to him physically, but also mentally. She loved the way he talked and the things he said. She felt like she could talk to him for hours about anything and everything. Just like they used to talk on the phone for hours and tell each other everything when they were kids. The chemistry was natural back then just like it was now. And now that she was grown and had experienced life, relationships, and love, she knew Junior was her man.

"Can I ask you something, Junior?"

He pulled the truck to a stop at the red light before turning to look at her. There was seriousness in her green eyes. "Yeah. You can ask me anything."

"We never got the opportunity to be with each other when we were kids. But now that we're grown, we can do whatever we want. If you don't have nothing to do, I want to take the rest of the day off to be with you."

He stared into her beautiful hypnotizing eyes a moment longer, trying to think of the right words to say. But no words could fully capture and express what he was feeling at the moment. So he leaned over and let his actions do the talking. Larena read his body and met him halfway. They didn't ease into the first kiss like most first-time kissers. Instead, they closed their eyes and allowed their hunger for one another to lead the way. Their tongues danced as their lips smacked. Hands found body parts and rubbed and squeezed. Pleasure moans escaped from throats. And before either of them knew what was happening, Larena climbed across the seat and onto Junior's lap and began grinding on him as they kissed passionately. Junior could feel his dick growing in his pants as he palmed her ass. And that's when the car horn began beeping.

"Oh shit!" Larena giggled as she locked eyes with the angry driver that sat behind them at the red light. "He big mad."

Junior burst out laughing when he looked through the rear-view mirror and saw the driver's angry mug and hand gestures. "Yeah. He pissed."

Larena climbed back over in the passenger seat and started laughing.

"What's funny?" he asked as he pulled away from the light.

"If I didn't have these jeans on, I woulda tore you off at that stoplight," she laughed.

Junior turned to look at her. Larena was super bad. Every nigga's Woman Crush Wednesday all seven days of the week. And the spontaneity that she just showed by jumping on his lap in the middle of traffic told him she knew how to get hers. "Call your job and take the rest of the day off."

Larena kept eye contact with him as she pulled out her phone and dialed a number. "Hey, Jim. My daughter is really sick and I need to take the rest of the day off so I can take her to the hospital. Can you cover for me?"

"Yeah. Sure. Take care of the baby."

"Thanks. See you tomorrow," she said, continuing to look him in the eyes as she made another call. "Hey, Jasmine. I need a favor. I might be working late tonight, so I need you to keep Kamari a little later."

"Yeah, cuz. Do your thing. I got her."

"Okay. Thanks, girl."

After ending the call, she sat her phone on the dashboard and leaned across the seat, unzipping Junior's pants. "I felt it when I was on top of you. Let me see it."

She freed him from his boxers and began stroking him up and down with her hand. Then she crawled over and kissed his neck and sucked on his earlobe while whispering nasty things in his ear. "My pussy is so muthafuckin' wet, Junior. I want to fuck you so bad. I want you to fuck me hard. Beat this pussy up, nigga! You hear me? Beat this pussy up!"

"I'mma beat that pussy up!" Junior promised, loving how she was turning him on.

Then she lowered her head in his lap and wrapped her juicy lips around his pole and sucked him hard.

"Oh, shit!" Junior moaned, gripping the steering wheel tightly, loving the lip service.

Larena went back and forth between giving him head and jacking him off while whispering nasty shit in his ear. When he came, she lowered her head and caught every drop of cum. Junior was so turned on and wanted to fuck so bad that he decided take her to the nearest place where they could be alone. That ended up being his stash spot. As soon as the door was locked, they attacked each other. Clothing was thrown off and they were naked in less than a minute. Junior shoved her onto the couch, checking out her body while he positioned himself between her thighs. Her breasts were big and firm with large areolas the color of chocolate milk. Her waist was small, hips wide, and pussy clean shaved. He didn't even think about a condom as he sat the head of his dick against her lips and pushed inside. Her insides were tight, wet, and hot.

"Ohh!" Larena moaned, gripping his hips as he dove deep into her guts.

"You want me to beat this pussy up?" he asked when their pelvises were touching.

Lust and pleasure swirled in Larena's green eyes as she stared up at him. "Beat it up," she whispered.

Junior lowered his head and began kissing her while bucking his hips. Larena lifted her hips to match him stroke for stroke while moaning in his mouth and kissing him. After a few minutes of missionary, Larena wanted more.

"Hit it harder, Junior! Hit it harder!"

He leaned back and grabbed her legs, pushing them all the way back until her knee caps were next to her ears. Then he crouched over her and drilled her with everything he had.

"Oh shit! Oh my god! Oh shit!" Larena screamed, loving the pleasure and pain.

He fucked her fast and hard until she started screaming that she was cumming.

"I'm cumming, Junior! Oh shit, I'm cumming!"

Her screams of pleasure were music to his ears, giving him the stamina and energy to keep going. After the waves of pleasure finished flowing through her body, they moved to the floor. Larena got on her hands and knees, and he rubbed and squeezed her light-skinned phatty as he got behind her. Then he slipped inside and gave her part two of the dick down. Larena continued to match his stroke, throwing her ass back at him. Their sweat-slicked bodies slapped every time his pelvis met her bouncing booty.

"Damn, yo' pussy good as fuck!" Junior groaned, loving the feel of her womb.

"So is yo' dick, Junior. Damn, nigga. Pull my hair."

He reached out and grabbed her ponytail, tugging until her face was pointed toward the ceiling.

"Yeah, nigga! Oh yeah! Now slap my ass!"

Junior slapped the right cheek and back handed the left cheek repeatedly while fucking her hard and pulling her hair. When she came a second time, he joined her. Then he fell on top of her, both of them breathing heavily.

"Damn, Junior. I knew we had crazy chemistry, but I didn't know it would be like this," she moaned. "I can't believe I came two times."

"I can. And I hope you don't think that was it," he said while gripping her ass.

She rolled on top of him, straddling his waist and staring into his eyes. "Who you think you talking to, nigga? I can fuck all night. Can you?"

"Not only can I fuck all night, I can fuck for days."

The sex-starved couple continued sexing all over the apartment until they were exhausted. When done, they lay on the couch, kissing.

"Do you got something to eat in here?" Larena asked. "I worked up an appetite."

"Hell nah. But I'm hungry too. Let's take a shower and then go eat."

Larena gave him one more kiss before getting up. "I love shower sex. You think you got one more in you?"

"I told you I can go for days," Junior said while sitting up.

"Show me." She grinned before heading toward the bathroom.

Junior was about to follow her but stopped when his phone rang. He had ignored it while they were sexing, but now he decided to check the calls. There were several missed calls from action and a couple text messages. The text that made him freeze was from John.

'S'n'lo dead. Hit me back.'

J-Blunt

Chapter 6

After reading the text, Junior's insides went numb. For a moment, he found it hard to complete a thought. When the information finally sank in, he hit up John on Facetime.

"S'n'Lo really dead?" he asked, unable to comprehend his nigga being gone.

The darkness in John's eyes told the truth before the words left his mouth. "Man, Junior. They got our nigga."

Junior just stared at his brother's face for a moment as the truth sank in. "What the fuck happened? Who did it?"

"Don't nobody know nothing right now. Some people sayin' he got set up by a bitch. Other mu'fuckas saying niggas was hating. Right now, don't nobody know."

Junior shook his head. "A'ight. I'm on my way to the hood. Where you at?"

"We all posted in front of Mom's house."

"A'ight. I'm on my way."

After ending the call, Junior let out a frustrated breath and closed his eyes as memories of S'n'Lo flooded his brain. They met when they were twelve years old and had been tight ever since. He remembered stealing cars and joy riding with his nigga. When they started hustling, they stopped stealing cars and gave their customers drugs to rent their cars for days and weeks. Junior quit school after coming home one day and seeing S'n'Lo with 3,500 dollars that he made during school hours. They had a major impact on each other's lives, and now his nigga was gone.

"What's taking you so long?" Larena asked, poking her head out of the bathroom.

Junior opened his eyes and just stared at her, trying to find the words. "I just found out my nigga dead."

Larena's eyes grew wide. "Who was it? What happened?"

"My nigga S'n'Lo. Don't nobody know what happened. I need to go to the hood."

"Okay. I just need a quick shower and you can drop me off at my cousin's daycare."

After a quick shower and dropping Larena off, Junior headed to Parklawn. There was a large crowd of his niggas and family members standing in front of his mother's house. "What's the word? Do they know who killed Lo?" Junior asked as he climbed from the truck.

"They still saying some shit about a set up," Fifty said.

"Where it happen at? Who was he with?"

"He was with some lil' bitch down on Ring. She said some nigga just walked up to him and shot him in the face," Toe Tagga said.

"That shit sound personal. It sound like a hit," Lo-Dog spoke up.

"Yeah," Black agreed. "Whoever did it wanted to make sure he was dead. Plus, they didn't take shit. It wasn't a robbery."

"Do anybody know who he had beef with?" Junior asked.

"Call Ricky Blow. Them niggas was always together. Maybe he know," John said.

As if on cue, Ricky Blow's red Porsche truck turned onto the block.

"There that nigga go right there," T-Murda pointed.

The Porsche pulled up behind Junior's Lexus. Ricky Blow hopped out wearing the grief on his tear-stained face. "They killed my nigga, y'all," he mourned.

"Who did it?" Fifty asked.

"These bitch ass CSG niggas. Niggas over on Clarke. The bitch who he was on Ring with used to fuck with one of them niggas. I told Lo to quit fucking with that bitch, but he wouldn't listen," Ricky Blow explained.

"How you know it was the CSG niggas?" Junior asked.

"The nigga name is T-Dog. A tall, skinny nigga with blond dreads. The bitch gotta baby by him. Nigga said some shit like if niggas fucking with his bitch, they gon' get bodied. Some bitch ass shit like that. Then my nigga get burned while he out with the bitch. I know it was T-Dog."

"Who is the bitch and where the bitch at now?" Lo-Dog asked.

"Bitch name is Lisaray. I don't know where she at right now, but she from over on 38th and Clarke. Live in a white house with a field next to it."

Fifty, Junior, and Lo-Dog shared looks.

"Is we riding for our nigga?" Fifty asked.

"You already know." Junior nodded.

Fifty looked at Lo-Dog.

"You ain't even gotta ask me, nigga," Lo-Dog mugged. "That was my lil' nigga. I'll kill all them CSG niggas. Every single one."

Fifty and Junior jumped in Lo-Dog's Challenger and drove over to 38th and Clarke. It was a little after five o'clock in the evening, and the block was alive with activity. Kids played in front of houses, people were sitting on porches enjoying the summer weather, and niggas were posted on corners or gathered around cars.

"That's the house right there," Lo-Dog said, pointing at a white house in the middle of the block with a field next to it.

"Pull over. I'm finna go see if she in there," Fifty said.

"Hold on, nigga! What you doing? It's too many people outside," Junior said, refusing to let his nigga catch a body in broad daylight.

"I just wanna see if the bitch is here so I know what she look like," Fifty said, tucking a fat ass 9 mm Desert Eagle in the front of his pants. "I'mma just make up some shit to get them to open the door. Y'all watch these niggas out here."

Lo-Dog held a Draco on his lap. "You know I got you, fool."

Junior clutched his Ruger while taking a look around. "We got you."

When Fifty hopped out the car, the Parklawn killers watched up and down the block for anything that looked suspicious.

"How long we gon' do this no talk shit, lil' cuz?" Lo-Dog asked.

"Ain't no time limit. You foul, nigga. That shit you did ain't cool."

"You act like it was just me. She approached me with that shit. How you gon' still fuck with her but not me?"

"Me and her gotta baby, nigga. That's my baby mama."

Lo-Dog raised his voice. "And we blood, nigga! Our mothers are sisters. We grew up together and spilled blood together. You telling me that the love you got for a bitch that came at me on some fuck shit is more than the love you got for a nigga that killed for you?"

Junior was silent, watching Fifty walk up on the porch and knock on the door. Then he turned to look at Lo-Dog, the pain of betrayal showed in his eyes. "You betrayed me, cuz. I didn't think you would do that to me. Outta all the fam, I never thought it would be you. Like you said, we spilled blood together. You was there the first time I shot a pistol. When Six went up north, I came to you for advice. You was my nigga, cuz. That's why that shit hurt so bad. I never thought it would be you."

"Look, cuz. I know what I did was foul. But we niggas. You like my lil' brother. I wasn't thinking clear at the time, my nigga. My bad, cuz. For real. I'm sorry, my nigga. I won't never do that bullshit again. That's my word. Fuck with me, cuz. I love you, lil' nigga."

Junior could see remorse in his cousin's eyes. He couldn't be mad at his nigga no more. Especially since he forgave Quitta. "We good, fam."

Lo-Dog extended his hand. They shook. Then movement on Lisaray's porch made the cousins get on point. Fifty and a nigga with blond dreads looked like they were exchanging words.

"What he on?" Junior asked, opening the door a little, ready to burn the nigga.

"Hold on, cuz. Let him handle it," Lo-Dog said, calming Junior but keeping his finger on the Draco's trigger.

They watched as Fifty lifted his hands in a peaceful gesture and back pedaled down the stairs. The blond-haired nigga said a couple more words before closing the door. Fifty walked back to the car smiling.

"Ooh, I'm killing that bitch ass nigga!" Fifty laughed as he got back in the car.

"Was that T-Dog?" Junior asked.

"He didn't say his name, but that was him. I knocked on the door and asked for the bitch, and that bitch ass nigga came out like he was on that," Fifty explained as Lo-Dog drove away. "I told the nigga I met the bitch a couple days ago, and he got on some super tough ass sucka shit. Talking 'bout, don't come by the house no more or he gon' body me. Ooh, I'm killing that bitch ass nigga tonight!"

***

When the sun went down, Fifty, Lo-Dog, and Junior were back on 38th and Clarke. They parked a stolen Jeep a block over and crept up to the house dressed in black and wearing COVID-19 face masks. They moved quickly around the house, keeping their guns out while looking in the windows to see how many people were inside. Problem was, all the windows were covered. When they realized they wouldn't be able to see inside, they gathered in the backyard.

"We gon' have to pull a kick door and run in blazing shit," Fifty said.

Junior didn't like the plan. It was too reckless. "What if we act like we the police? If we try to kick the door in, they gon' start shooting. If we say we the police, they might not."

Lo-Dog smiled. "That's the play. Let's go."

They walked to the back door and Junior began banging loudly. "Milwaukee Police Department! We have a search warrant!" Lo-Dog and Fifty began kicking the door violently. Three kicks later, the door crashed open. Junior ran in the house, letting the Ruger lead the way. Lo-Dog and Fifty followed. They entered through the kitchen and spotted a back room.

"I got it," Junior said, kicking the door open and pointing the gun at the bed. A little girl sat up and began screaming. Junior paused, unsure of what to do. Gunshots from somewhere in the house made him snap back to the moment. He closed the door and moved toward the front of the house. Lisara lay on the floor bleeding from bullet holes in her chest. A man lay a few feet away with a chunk of his face missing.

"Was anybody back there?" Lo-Dog asked.

Junior shook his head. "Nah. Just a baby."

"You sure?" Fifty asked. "This ain't the nigga from earlier."

Junior took another look at the nigga with part of his face missing. It wasn't T-Dog. "Yeah. It's a little girl in bed. That nigga gotta be gone. Let's get the fuck outta here."

They were headed toward the back of the house when Lo-Dog stopped. "Hold on," he whispered, walking toward the back room. "Y'all heard that?"

"That's the shorty," Junior said.

Lo-Dog shook his head, standing on the side of the door and listening. Junior knew the kid was in the room, so he walked over, reaching for the knob and twisting. Lo-Dog shoved him out of the way as gunshots rang out.

Clap, clap, clap, clap, clap, clap, clap, clap, clap!

Junior fell to the floor as the bullets tore through the door. He had almost become a corpse. Lo-Dog saved his life. Fifty and Lo-Dog also returned fire at the room.

Brrrreeeaaaaattt! Brrrreeeaaaaattt! Brrrreeeaaaaattt!

Pop, pop, pop, pop, pop, pop, pop, pop!

When the shooting stopped, a man could be heard moaning in pain.

"Daddy! Daddy!" the little girl screamed.

Junior got up from the floor and pointed his gun at the door. Lo-Dog stayed hidden behind the wall and pushed the door open. When no one started shooting, Fifty and Junior peeked into the room. T-Dog was on the floor, back against the wall. A pistol was on the floor a few feet away. There were several bullet holes in his body, but he was still alive. The little girl lay on the floor near the closet unharmed.

"Got yo' bitch ass," Fifty chuckled as he walked in the room. He lifted the Desert Eagle to T-Dog's face and ended his life.

Pop!

Lo-Dog stood over the little girl and aimed the Draco.
"Nah, cuz!" Junior screamed.
Brrrreeeaaaaattt!

***

Quitta sat up in bed watching Junior sleep. He had come home late again and she was tired of it. For more than a month he had been coming home at two or three o'clock in the morning, sleeping until nine or ten, and then was back out again. It seemed like the only time she saw him was when he was sleeping. He always said he was hustling, but she knew better. Selling drugs didn't mean he had to come home late. He sold drugs while they lived in Lacrosse and he was always home at night. He tried to tell her that selling rock was different from heroin, but she wasn't going for that bullshit. Hustling was hustling, no matter what was being sold. And the fact that they hadn't had sex in almost three weeks didn't make the situation any better. Junior was cheating on her and she knew it. Her intuition told her so. She knew her man, and one thing she knew about Junior was he loved to fuck. And if he wasn't getting it from her, he was getting it from somewhere else.

She thought about waking him up by busting him in his shit, but she didn't want to do anything that could lead to somebody calling the police. Her picture was all on the news, and the last thing she needed was unwanted attention. That was another problem. The police. It was only a matter of time before they found out who she was. Junior said he had enough money to bail her out and get a lawyer, but that didn't give her much comfort. A lawyer and bail money didn't mean she wasn't going to be charged with murder or end up in prison. The thought of her son being raised by another woman was devastating. Junior said he would wait on her if she went to jail, but he was lying. If he cheated on her while she was free, things would only become worse when she was gone. The real question she needed to ask herself was should she take a case for a nigga that wasn't being faithful? Part of her said yes. Another part said no. She didn't know which part to listen to. What she really needed was evidence. If she could find proof whether or not he was cheating, that would make her decision easier. She grabbed his phone and went to the bathroom. After sitting on the toilet, she began searching his call log. She recognized some of the numbers as friends and family. The ones that she didn't know, she called. She began at the top and pressed call.

"Junior, what's good, my boy?" a man answered.

Quitta hung up and dialed another number. Whenever a man answered, she hung up. If a woman answered, Quitta found out who she was and her relationship with Junior. She had dialed about ten numbers when she came up on the name L. She called the number, expecting L to be a man.

"Hey, baby!" a woman answered.

Hearing the woman's voice and "baby" made Quitta flinch. "Who is this?"

There was a pause.

"Hello?" the woman asked.

"Who are you, lady?" Quitta asked, feeling her body growing hot with anger.

"Wow," the woman chuckled. "Is this Quitta?"

"Yeah, this me, bitch. Who the fuck is you? And how the fuck you know my name?"

"Wait, Quitta. We don't gotta do the bitch thing. My name is Larena. Junior told me who you are."

Quitta laughed, shaking her head. She had found the other woman. " Okay, Larena. How do you know Junior?"

"I've been knowing Junior since we were twelve years old. His cousin, Patricia, is my friend," she answered calmly.

"And what do you know about me?"

"You're his son's mother."

"Are you fucking my man?" Quitta asked, getting to the point.

"That's a conversation you need to have with 'your man.'"

The way she said 'your man' spoke volumes. It meant she held some type of attachment to Junior and some jealousy toward Quitta.

"I'm talking to you right now. Woman to woman. Did you fuck Junior?"

Larena paused again. "Whatever I do with Junior is between me and Junior. I don't owe you loyalty. He does. That's a conversation you need to have with your man, boo."

Quitta became livid. "I'm not yo' boo, punk ass bitch! You need to be ashamed of yo'self for fucking a nigga with a family. It's hoes like you that ruin families. You nasty ass, cum bucket ass bitch. If I ever see you, I'm beating yo' ass!"

"Bitch, I ain't worried about you," Larena swore, finally losing her cool. "And I know you ain't talking about ruining families. I heard about you fucking Lo-Dog. How you gon' fuck yo' man cousin but call me nasty? You the nasty bitch."

The dig cut Quitta to the heart. She needed to get even, so she swung low. "Since yo' bitch ass know everything, did you know that Junior got herpes, bitch? Bet yo' ass didn't know that, did you?"

"Junior got herpes?!" Larena asked, her voice high pitched with alarm.

Banging on the bathroom door prevented Quitta from responding.

"Quitta, you got my phone?" Junior yelled from the hallway.

"You heard what I said, bitch. Ask him," Quitta said before snatching the door open. She threw the phone into Junior's chest, making him stumble into the wall. "Talk to yo' bitch and get the fuck outta my house, nigga!" she yelled before taking a swing. Junior was barely able to dodge the first punch, but he couldn't dodge the second one. It landed right on his nose, making his eyes watery. After catching his balance, he checked his nose for blood. Sure enough, there was blood on his fingers. And Quitta was gone.

Damn, this bitch just bust my nose! he thought.

He looked down and picked his phone up from the floor. When he saw the L on the screen, he already knew shit was fucked up. He didn't even bother trying to talk to Larena. Instead, he ended the call and put the phone in his pocket. Right now, his only concern was giving Quitta a matching bloody nose.

"Where the fuck you at, bitch!?" he yelled, heading for the bedroom.

Quitta stood near the bed panicking. She didn't know what to do. She punched him and knew he would want his lick back. When she saw his bloody face and angry eyes, she knew he was about to attack her. So she picked up the closest thing to her to defend herself. It was the laptop. She held it over her head while walking backward. "Get the fuck away from me, nigga! I knew you was cheating on me! Get out!"

Junior kept walking toward her. "Put that computer down, bitch! Look what the fuck you did to my nose!"

Quitta realized there was no way around him and he wasn't going to stop. So she threw the computer at him and tried to run. Junior dodged the computer and chased her around the bed. He grabbed her by the back of the hair and snatched her onto the bed. Quitta tucked into a tight ball and covered her face as he climbed on top of her.

"Punk ass bitch!" Junior cursed as he rained down blows to Quitta's head, arms, and hands. He tried to pry her hands from her face so he could bust her nose, but she remained curled in a tight ball.

"Daddy, what you doing to Mama!?" Mooka screamed.

Junior looked up and saw his son standing in the doorway with tears in his eyes. As bad as he wanted to fuck Quitta up, he wasn't going to do it in front of their son. So he climbed off Quitta and went to the bathroom to wash the blood from his face and stop the bleeding. While he was washing his face, the phone rang. It was Larena.

"Hello?"

"She said you got herpes, nigga! You got herpes!?" Larena screamed.

"What the fuck is you talking about?" Junior asked, sitting the phone on the sink.

"Quitta said you have herpes! I swear to God, you bet not have burned me, nigga!"

"Man, I don't got no muthafuckin' herpes. She lied. But I can't talk right now. I'mma holla at you later."

After cleaning up and stopping his nose from bleeding, Junior went back to the room to get dressed. He grabbed a red Louis Vuitton fit and threw it on.

Quitta was standing in the corner with a knife in one hand and Mooka in her arms. "Get the fuck outta my house, nigga! I knew yo' bitch ass was cheating on me."

"Yeah, I cheated. So what. If yo' ass wasn't so crazy and insecure, I wouldn't have no reason to cheat. You made me do it."

"Nigga, that shit sound stupid as hell. You cheated because you wanted to. Because you not a man. You a punk ass little boy. And I don't want no lil' boys. Go to yo' mama house, lil' boy."

Junior laughed at her before grabbing his money and a pistol. "I hope you can bail out and get yo' own lawyer. Don't call me for shit. Fuck you, bitch."

The thought of no bail or lawyer scared the shit out of Quitta, but she wasn't about to let it show. "Fuck you and your money, Junior! You gon' get yours. I promise you that."

Junior left home and went to the stash apartment to drop off the money and think of his next move. He was still mad about Quitta going through his phone and busting his nose. When his phone buzzed, he checked and saw a text from Quitta. She threatened him and cussed him out. After reading the text, he grabbed the last G sack and left the apartment to get some weed to calm his nerves.

"What's good, brah?" John answered, still sounding sleepy.

"What's up, nigga? You got some weed?"

"Yeah," he yawned. "Where you at?"

"I'm on my way to you. You at Nikki house?"

"Yeah. Come through."

Twenty minutes later, Junior parked outside an apartment building right off Sherman and Villard. He rang the doorbell for apartment four and waited. A few moments later, the door opened and he was greeted by a pretty dark-skinned woman with a humongous booty.

"What's good, Junior?" She smiled.

"Nikki, what's good, baby?"

"I'm good. C'mon in. John in the shower."

Junior followed her big booty down the hall and into the apartment.

"Have a seat. You want something to drink?" she offered.

"Nah, I'm good on that drink. Where the weed at? John said he had some."

"I'mma go look. I'mma be right back."

Junior sat down and went through his phone. There was another threatening text from Quitta and another text from his cousin, Patricia. He decided to call her back.

"What's up, cuz?"

"Hey, Junior. Uh, Larena called me and said Quitta told her you got herpes. What's going on?"

"Man, Quitta lied. I don't got no fucking herpes. She went through my phone while I was sleeping and called Larena."

"Yeah, I told her Quitta was probably lying. So, how you doing? Are you good?"

Junior touched his nose instinctively. "Yeah, I'm good. Probably gotta find somewhere to stay for a couple of days."

"Well, if you need my help, let me know. I'm at work so I can't talk right now. And call Larena. She freaking out a little bit."

"A'ight. I'mma call her later," he said before hanging up.

Nikki came into the living room a few moments later. "Here go some weed and a wrap."

"Hell yeah," Junior said gladly, grabbing the weed and rolling up.

"Why you up so early?" Nikki asked as she sat down and turned on the TV.

"Shit, it's damn near nine thirty. I'm always up this early."

Nikki laughed.

"What's funny?"

"I wasn't eavesdropping, but I heard some of your call. Did Quitta really do you like that? Told a bitch you had herpes?"

Junior shook his head. "Ain't that some bullshit?"

"Yeah, that is. But if it was me, I'dda told the bitch you had full blown AIDS," she laughed.

Junior shook his head and lit the blunt.

"I'm just sayin', Junior. I ain't with that cheating shit. If your brother cheats on me, I'mma cut that nigga dick off. Bet he won't be fucking nobody else."

Junior winced. "Damn, you scandalous!"

"Who fucking who?" John asked, walking into the living room.

"You bet not be fucking nobody, nigga. She in here talking about cutting yo' dick off, nigga," Junior said.

John mugged Nikki. "Fuck you talking 'bout?"

"Junior got caught cheating and Quitta told the bitch he had herpes. I told him if you ever cheated on me, I'm cutting off yo' dick. Snip, snip, nigga," she said, using her hands like scissors

John's eyes popped. "Quitta caught you? On what?"

"She didn't catch me in the act. She went through my phone while I was sleeping and called Larena. Told her I had herpes."

John bust out laughing. "Damn, sis crazy! On what, she called Larena, though? Damn."

"Stupid ass shit. Some shit I don't got time for. I'm try'na get a bag. What you on? I'm finna hit the block."

"Shit, I'm with you," he said before turning to his girl. "I'm 'bout to slide with bro. I'mma be back later."

Nikki stood to give him a hug. "Alright. I'm going out with my sister later. I'mma call you. And you bet not be out there giving my dick away," she said while palming his crotch.

John gripped two handfuls of her big ass booty as they shared a sloppy kiss. "I ain't giving away nothing that belongs to you as long as you don't give away nothing that belongs to me."

"Okay then. See you later."

When the brothers were outside, John got on Junior again. "I can't believe you got caught cheating, nigga. Why you don't got two phones? One for the action and the other one for the hoes."

"Man, I don't be thinking about that shit. Plus, I didn't think she would go through my phone."

"Hoes is sneaky, my nigga. You can't trust 'em. That's like the bitch upstairs. Bad lil' vibe name Anita. Got a nigga and everything. And she tight with Nikki. But the bitch be letting me come through and stick long dick all down her tonsils."

Junior shook his head as they climbed in the Lexus truck. "You playing with fire, nigga. The bitch live upstairs and she got a nigga. You must not want to have kids."

John waved Junior off. "I wish that bitch would try some shit like that. I'll bury her ass somewhere where won't nobody find her."

The brothers shared a laugh. Junior drove to the hood and parked in front of his mother's house. They were climbing from the truck when a police car turned onto the block. Junior saw them immediately. He had a G sack in his pocket and pistol on his hip. The last thing he needed was police contact.

"Twelve," John warned.

"Walk toward the house," Junior said, leading the way.

They were walking up the walkway when the police car accelerated. Then it came to a screeching stop in front of the Lexus truck, and two cops hopped out.

"Hey! You in the red shirt! Stop!"

Junior glanced over his shoulder and saw them reaching for their guns. No way he was about to be caught with dope and a pistol. Not when he still had three years of parole. So he took off running. He ran through the backyard and the cops chased, ignoring John. He ran through the alley, tossing the gun in the bushes, and kept on running through the yard across the alley. He glanced back and saw he had a good lead on the cops as he sprinted across the street. He dashed through another yard and threw the drugs in the backseat of a car that was in the driveway. He ran across another alley and through another yard. He looked over his shoulder again and saw the cops still chasing.

"Fuck!" he cursed as his chest began burning.

He ran through another yard and was crossing the street when he saw another cop car speeding toward him. He locked eyes with the cop driving as the car tried to ram him. He barely dodged the car and was about to run through another yard but stopped when he saw a pit bull. When he looked behind him, the cops were pulling their guns.

"Get on the mutherfucking ground, right now!"

Junior looked back at the yard and was about to jump the gate until he saw another pit bull barking and charging the gate. No way he was about to try two pit bulls.

"Bitch ass shit!" he cursed as he lay face down in the grass.

***

Junior sat in the holding cell staring at the wall, thoughts running wild. The cops said they got an anonymous tip that somebody wearing red clothing and fitting his description had a gun. He wasn't sure if they were lying or telling the truth. The police always used the excuse that a nigga fit the description. But he also couldn't shake the look in Quitta's eyes when she said he was going to get his. Something in his gut told him she had called the police and given the anonymous tip. But another part of him couldn't believe it. Was she really that shiesty that she would send him to jail and possibly ruin her chance at getting bail and lawyer money to fight her case? Nobody could be that stupid, could they? It just didn't make sense.

"Fuck," he cursed, letting out a deep and frustrated breath.

He also couldn't believe he was locked up again. Not only did he have three years of parole hanging over his head, but the police also found the dope inside the car and said it was his. The cells in Dodge Correctional Institution flashed through his head. He had almost made it. He was one move away from being plugged in with some real bosses. He wondered why movies and books always had the character getting killed or locked up right before they made their power move. *Damn, that shit was too real.* And then there was Fredo. Quitta's picture had been shown on the news as a person of interest and he had been in the club with her. Did the police have him listed as a person of interest too? Was this about more than the dope charge?

A key being inserted into the lock got his attention. The door opened, and a female officer wearing a facemask stuck her head inside. "The detectives want to talk to you. Cuff up."

After being cuffed, he was led through the jail and to an interrogation room. "They'll be with you in a minute," she said before taking the cuffs off and leaving.

Junior looked around the small room as he waited to be interrogated. He already knew the rules. Don't say shit. Ask for a lawyer. And don't say shit! The door opened a few minutes later, and in walked the last person on earth he wanted to see. "Small fucking world, ain't it, Junior?" Detective Johnson grinned.

Junior shook his head. "I don't got nothing to say. I want a lawyer."

"Did Gail teach you that? Because she said the same damn thing right before we tried to question your sister. Them damn apples don't fall too far from those muthafuckin' trees, huh?" He grinned, showing every tooth in his mouth.

Junior didn't respond.

Detective Johnson slapped him on the arm like they were buddies as he sat in a chair on the other side of the table. "Cheer up, Junior. Damn. This ain't no funeral, nigga. This is the best thing that could've ever happened to you. Ask me why? C'mon, now. Ask me."

Junior humored him. "Why?"

The detective stopped smiling, giving him a serious look. "'Cause I'm gon' bust yo' ass, Junior. You hear me, nigga? I'mma bust yo' ass wide open like a tranny in a prison shower," he cracked before busting out laughing.

Junior didn't find the joke funny.

"Okay, kid. Let me tell you what's going on," he said, becoming serious again. "The officers got a call that somebody on 47th Street dressed in red had a gun. Just so happens that the officers turn on the block and see you. When they try to question you, you run. Lucky for you, they didn't find the gun. Otherwise, I'd be greasing yo' asshole with Vaseline." He smiled, making Junior uncomfortable with his homosexual humor. "But they did find some two hundred rocks in a car that you ran by. Since that wasn't your car, the case probably won't stick. I thought about sending it to the lab and doing some fingerprinting or DNA matches, but this COVID shit got the whole world and the court system moving in slow motion. So, that works in yo' favor. They only taking the big, serious cases. An ounce of crack ain't all that serious. So, today is yo' lucky day, Junior. You not about to be charged for the dope that I'm pretty sure was yours. Now, what do you say?" he asked, smiling again.

"Can I leave?" Junior asked.

His smile disappeared. "No, you cannot leave. We still got a little more talking to do."

Fredo's dead body laying in the gas station parking lot flashed in Junior's head.

"About what? The dope ain't mine."

The detective looked him in the eyes for a couple of long and agonizing seconds. "We need to talk about Terrance Brooks." Junior was surprised to hear the name. How in the hell did Detective Johnson know about Terrance?

"Who is that?" he asked with no conviction.

Detective Johnson burst out laughing. "Nigga, you don't even believe that you don't know him. You know damn well who Terrance is, Junior. Weren't you living in Lacrosse, Wisconsin about two months ago?"

Junior panicked on the inside but tried to look calm. "Man, where is my lawyer?"

"You don't need a lawyer right now. We just talking. I don't got a notepad or recorder. This is just me and you talking. That's it. You did know Terrance, right? 'Cause there are some people up north saying you and Terrance were super tight."

Junior shrugged. "I knew a lot of people in Lacrosse."

"That's the truest thing that you said since you been sitting in that chair," the detective said and began staring at Junior again. "So, I'm working with the Lacrosse Police Department to bring you up on some real charges, Junior. Yeah, we probably gonna end up locking up your whole family. We already got your sister. You're next.

What was your other sister's name that was sitting on the couch with your mother? Yeah, we're gonna get her ass too. The whole family." He smiled.

Junior remained silent. Detective Johnson was out to take down his entire family. The last thing he needed to do was add fuel to the fire.

"Well, that's all I got for you, kid," the detective said as he stood. "I coulda called your parole officer and got you held for thirty days for running from those patrolmen, but I didn't. I'm not that petty. When I get you, I'mma get you good. Send that ass back up north with football numbers. So go on out there and sell some more drugs and make it easy for me. I'll send an officer in to release you. See you soon."

***

Junior had never been scared of the police before, but Detective Johnson had him spooked. Not only was the nigga crazy, but he also had some kind of crush on Junior, and the shit made him feel weird. After getting his property, he called John to come pick him up. During the ride, he told his little brother everything that happened in the interrogation room.

"What the fuck, brah? The nigga gay and he try'na lock you up? You think he was try'na do some favor for a favor type shit?" John asked.

"Man, I don't know. All I know is this bitch ass nigga coming. He talking about locking up everybody."

The brothers were silent for a moment. Thinking.

"Did he say why they swooped down on you? Why the fuck they was looking for you? Did he send 'em?"

Junior shook his head. "Nah. I think Quitta did that shit."

John's eyes popped. "Yeah right! You think Quitta tried to get you knocked!?"

Junior nodded. "They said they got an anonymous tip that a nigga dressed in red had a gun. Quitta knew what I had on."

John wasn't convinced. "I don't think sis would send you to jail, my nigga. That shit would make it harder on her. Plus, I seen when you threw the banger and went and grabbed it. They came back looking for it too."

Junior smiled at his little brother. "On what, you grabbed it? Good looking, nigga! They was sho' try'na bam me."

"Hell yeah. I got you, nigga. But is you sure Quitta did it, my nigga? That's some serious shit."

"I don't know what to think, my nigga. I just remember that look in her eyes when she said I was gon' get what I had coming. She wanted revenge for me try'na beat her ass this morning, my nigga. And I already know she would do anything to get back at me and hurt me. That's why she fucked Lo-Dog."

John nodded. "You do got a point. But jail? I don't know."

Junior spent the rest of the day chilling at his mother's house. Detective Johnson had him scared to go out and hustle. Plus, he was still waiting on Six to come to town so he could get his seat at the table. Making it out of the police station was some kind of blessing, and the last thing he wanted to do was fuck up a good thing. Not wanting to risk getting in any trouble, he spent the day kicking it with his niggas, getting fucked up, and playing video games.

***

"Daddy, wake up! Wake up, Daddy."

Junior opened his eyes and saw Mooka's face inches away from his. "What's up, young money? What you doing over here?"

"Wake up, Daddy. Why you didn't come home?"

The smell of a cigarette made Junior look around the room. Quitta stood at the foot of the bed smoking.

"Me and Mama had a fight, so I stayed at Granny's house," he explained to his son.

Mooka turned to his mother. "Can Daddy come back home now? You not mad no more, right?"

"Go downstairs with Granny so I can talk to yo' daddy," Quitta said.

Mooka did as he was told. They waited until he was gone before speaking.

"Why didn't you spend the night with your girlfriend?" Quitta began.

Junior sat up on his elbows and mugged her. "Why the fuck you call the police on me, nigga?"

Quitta looked confused. "Nigga, what the fuck is you talking about?"

Junior studied her for a moment, looking for a sign that she was lying. Quitta kept a straight face, looking innocent.

"I got chased by the police after I left home. They said they got an anonymous tip that a nigga dressed in red had a gun. Now I got a bitch ass detective asking me questions about Terrance and talking about putting some grease in my ass."

Quitta looked confused. "Some grease in yo' ass? What that gotta do with Terrance? And how the fuck they know about Terrance?"

Junior leaned forward and grabbed Quitta's Newport and took a long pull. "I don't know. I think the nigga gay. He kept on saying gay ass shit. But I do know that he talked to the police in Lacrosse and they try'na build a case. Somebody must've told 'em I had something to do with him getting whacked. He knew that me and Terrance used to be cool."

Quitta moved closer to Junior, concern in her eyes. "Damn, baby daddy! What the fuck is going on? You want me to call Ron?"

He cut his eyes at her. "I want you to tell me why the fuck you called the police on me. I know it was you, nigga."

"Junior, I didn't call the police on you. Is you crazy? They looking for me. Why would I call them? I don't want you to go to jail."

"Because you a spiteful and vengeful muthafucka. That's why you fucked Lo-Dog."

Quitta's eyes turned dark with anger. "Yeah, because you fucked Nyla, nigga! That's my fucking sister in-law, nigga. And you told yo' little bitch that shit too, because she sure brought it up when I was talking to her. How the fuck you gon' cheat on me, nigga? I fuck you every kind of way. I suck yo' dick and swallow.

I do everything you want me to do. I thought you wasn't gon' do that shit no more. I thought we both learned from all the shit that happened in Lacrosse?"

Junior took another drag on the cigarette. "I had a weak moment. I felt like you was pushing me away."

Quitta got loud. "Yeah, because you staying out all night and cheating on me, nigga! What the fuck? You think I'm supposed to be happy about that shit?"

"I only cheated on you one time. That's my word."

"And one time is too many, nigga. We already went through this shit, Junior. Why the fuck would you do it again? That's some bullshit."

They became silent. When the cigarette was gone, Junior got up to throw it out the window.

"So, what is we doing, Junior? What's going on?"

He leaned against the dresser and stared at her. She tried to look all innocent, like she was the victim, but he knew better. He knew she called the police on him. He could feel it in his gut. And if she would do that, there was nothing she wouldn't do. If she would take his freedom, she would take his life. He couldn't trust her. And he couldn't be with nobody he couldn't trust. "I'mma stay at Mom's crib for a minute."

Quitta looked like he smacked her. "What? Why? And what is you saying?"

"I don't trust you, Quitta. I know you called the police on me, and I ain't finna be with nobody I can't trust. Ain't no telling what you would do."

"Ain't that about a bitch!" Quitta mugged him. "Nigga, you the one that cheated on me, and you got the nerve to talk about trust! Ain't that about a bitch! You know what, Junior? Fuck you, nigga. You saying this shit because you wanna keep fucking these nasty ass bitches. That's why you wanna stay with yo' mama. Just gimmie some money so I can get a fucking lawyer. Fuck you, nigga. I can't believe I put my life and freedom on the line for you, nigga."

"Just keep laying low. If they come for you, I'mma take care of everything. I got you."

Quitta looked like she wanted to say more but didn't. They were done talking. It was over. So she went downstairs and grabbed her son and went home.

Chapter 7

"I just got off the phone with Six. He said he gon' be in the city tonight," John announced as he walked in the apartment.

Junior, RIP, and T-Murda were all sitting around the living room in Jeff's apartment hustling and waiting for a word from Six so they could make their next move. RIP and T-Murda were playing Xbox. Junior had his face buried in his phone.

"That's what the fuck I'm talking 'bout." T-Murda smiled, rubbing his hands together like he was trying to warm them. "I'm ready to eat. Get that El Chapo plug!"

"Nigga, I'mma glide and ride Bentleys and Phantoms," John laughed, shaking T-Murda's hand. "We finna plug with the cartel. Get our shit fresh off the boat. Cocaine cowboys!"

"We need to come up with a name for our squad. We the Parklawn Crime Mob!" RIP said.

Junior finally looked up from his phone. "Nah, not the crime mob. Parklawn Gangstas."

"Hell nah. Both y'all shit is whack," John laughed. "Nigga, we the Parklawn Grind Squad."

The cousins all shared a look.

"Parklawn Grind Squad. PGS," RIP said, liking the way the words rolled off his tongue.

"Parklawn Grind Squad." T-Murda smiled. "Yeah, fam. We Parklawn Grinders, nigga!"

Junior nodded. " Parklawn Grinders! I like it."

"Who you caking with on that phone, nigga?" John asked, flopping down on the couch next to his brother. "Let me find out you begging Quitta to let you back in the house, nigga."

"Fuck you, nigga," Junior said, giving his little brother a playful shrug. "I'm too much of a playa to beg a bitch for anything. If anything, she begging me to come home, nigga."

"Okay, then. Talk that shit, big bro." John smirked. "You ever think about how we gon' take over Parklawn, though? Nigga, this four blocks of project buildings. Ain't nobody ever tried to lock it down. All the niggas that we grew up with out there on they own shit. How we gon' lock up a whole project?"

"We gotta State Property them niggas. Get down or lay down," RIP said.

"We can't kill everybody," T-Murda cut in, trying to be the voice of reason. "Plus, bodies gon' make the whole hood hot."

"Murda right," Junior said. "We can't shoot er'body and too many bodies gon' have twelve all in this bitch, and a nigga ain't gon' be able to get no money. We gon' make pistol play a last option. When the work drop, we gon' make our bags bigger. Whatever it is, rocks, food, loud, pills, we gon' give it away at first. Since niggas got coronavirus prices, they cheating everybody. Right now everything stepped on. When we give out more and charge the same amount with straight drop, we gon' take all the action. Then when the hustlers see that we really eating, we gon' bring a few of them niggas in and put them on. After we got it locked, we gon' slowly downsize the work back to the level the streets playing at but keep our shit drop. At first we might lose a little bit, but sometimes you gotta lose to win."

John nodded approvingly. "You been listening when Six been dropping them jewels, huh?"

"Stop playing, my nigga. You know I'm made of the same shit Six made of. The Game God gives wisdom liberally. All you gotta do is ask for it. I'm blessed."

"Fool ass nigga!" RIP laughed.

After giving the hustler's version of a sermon, Junior stood and headed for the door. "I gotta make a move. Send me a text if y'all holla at Six before I do."

"Don't put me out, don't put me out, don't put me out! Please, baby!" John mocked, singing the hook of the R. Kelly classic as Junior left.

After leaving Jeff's house, Junior hopped in the Lexus and got in traffic. Fifteen minutes later, he parked in front of a blue and white townhouse on 95th and Capitol. He sent a text before getting out and walking up on the porch. When the door opened, Larena greeted him with a smile bright enough to make the projects feel like a mansion. Her green eyes sparkled like emeralds, and she wore a yellow flower in her hair along with a yellow and white sundress.

"Hey, you."

"Hey. You know I gotta thing for a woman in a sundress." Junior grinned, wrapping her in a hug.

"So I've heard. C'mon in."

He stepped in the house and took a look around. There was a white staircase leading upstairs. To the left was the living room. Fluffy gray carpet, a black couch set, and end tables. A big screen on the wall. There were also lots of pictures of Larena, her daughter, and family. Junior picked up one of the pictures of Larena's daughter.

"She cute as hell. Look just like you."

"That's my mini me," Larena smiled. "I wish you could've met her, but she out with my sisters."

"Me too. I'mma have to introduce you to my lil' nigga, too. He my mini-me," Junior said as he sat the picture down.

"I seen pictures of him on Facebook. He look like the doctors cloned him. He has all of your features. He gon' be so handsome when he grows up,"

"Nigga gon' be stunting like his daddy," Junior cracked.

"You crazy," Larena laughed. "Sit down. Relax. I'mma go grab some drinks."

Junior grabbed the remote control as he sat down. He flipped through a few channels before stopping on a re-run of *Love After Lock Up*. Larena came back a few minutes later with a bottle of Hennessy, two glasses of ice, and a blunt.

"Ooh, I love this show!" she said while sitting the drinks on the table.

Junior reached for the blunt. "And I love how you treat your guests."

"Gotta set the night off right. Ain't nothing like a glass of Hennessy and a blunt after a long day of work."

"Preach to me, baby," Junior said before taking a big hit of the weed.

After making drinks, Larena handed him a glass and sat next to him. "So, what was up with your baby mama calling me on that bullshit?"

"Man, we been having problems ever since I started back hustling. She swore I was cheating because I was coming in the house late. That shit created all kinds of problems. But on my word, I wasn't fucking off. I was try'na run up a check. I gotta move in the works that can change our life. That's what I was on. But she didn't believe me."

"She sound like she was insecure."

"Maybe. I really don't know. But that shit drove us apart. Then a couple mornings ago, she went through my phone and called you," he said before passing her the weed.

Larena started laughing. "I was like, what the hell? I couldn't believe she called me. At first I was talking to her respectfully. I was trying to keep it classy, you know? I'm not with that extra shit. I wasn't gon' tell her that we fucked because that wasn't my place to tell her that. That's a conversation for you and her. I just wanted to let her know that we were friends. But when she told me that herpes shit, I was like what!? Oh, hell nah!"

Junior took a sip of henny and let out a chuckle. "That ain't even the worst part. I swear I think she called the police on me. I damn near got sent back up."

Larena's eyes popped. "Yeah right! What she call the police for?"

"Because she spiteful as a mu'fucka. Police pulled up on me at Mom's crib talking about I fit the description of a nigga wit' a gun. I'm dirty, so I had to run to get rid of everything. Luckily, John seen where I threw the pistol and grabbed it. If they woulda caught me with that shit, I'd be sitting in the county sick right now. Shit, just having police contact could get me locked up because I'm on parole."

"Don't she realize that if you go back to jail that will make it harder for her and your son?"

"That shit don't matter when a nigga want revenge. Plus, she still saying she didn't do it, but I know she did."

A light flashed in Larena's eye's. "I swear, I just think you need something better. A real woman. Somebody that will let you do your thing but also push you to be better. You one of the rare good niggas out here. You're a king. You should have a good woman. A queen. What do you think you deserve?"

Junior turned to look at Larena. He could see the desire for him in her eyes. She didn't just want him, she wanted to own and possess him. And that shit was sexy. He felt a connection to her that was deeper than attraction or lust. He wasn't sure if it was because of their connection as kids or something else altogether. All he knew was at that moment, the only place he wanted to be was wherever she was.

"I'mma king. I deserve a queen."

"Come and get me," she moaned before leaning into him.

Junior met her halfway, their lips meeting in an intensely passionate kiss. They kept their eyes open, the glint in her eyes matching his own. When their arousals were heightened, they paused long enough for him to sit the drink on the table, and she dropped the blunt in the ashtray. When their lips met again, Larena's kisses became more aggressive, her tongue plunging into his mouth as she climbed onto his lap, straddling him. She cradled his face in both hands while grinding on his lap. Her moans were like gasoline on Junior's fire. He pushed her onto the couch, grinding between her legs while exchanging kisses.

"Fuck me, Junior," Larena demanded.

He stood to take off his clothes while Larena slipped the sundress over her head, revealing no underwear or bra. With her legs open, she slipped a hand between her thighs and began stroking her kitten. He paused to watch her fingers rub the fleshy inner folds of her pussy. She moaned while making faces of pleasure, driving Junior crazy. When he couldn't stand to watch anymore, he moved forward, kneeling between her legs. His lips found hers at the same time that his dick penetrated. They kept their eyes open, her green eyes changing to gold as he plunged deep into her sugary walls. A small moan escaped her lips, and her hands dug into his back as he thrust in and out slowly. But Larena didn't want slow and steady.

She pushed her hips to meet his thrusts, saying with her body what her mouth filled with his tongue wouldn't let her say. And he understood her language, picking up his pace until he was drilling deep, fast, and hard.

"Oh shit! Oh god, Junior! Oh my god!" Larena cried, loving the pleasure and pain.

Junior kept up the pace, leaning back and lifting one of her legs so he could go deeper.

"Yes, Junior! Don't stop, nigga! Oh, don't stop!"

He didn't stop. He kept his hips moving as sweat began dripping down his body. He watched Larena's sex faces, caught up in her ecstasy. She was undoubtedly a beautiful woman, but her sex faces were the most beautiful thing he had ever seen. Watching her pleasure pushed him toward the edge. He could feel his explosion getting near, and there was no way in the world he was pulling out.

"Awe, shit!" he groaned, busting so hard he became light headed.

Junior paused above her as his dick spasmed inside her, fighting the pleasure and pain that paralyzed him. Larena pulled his face down to hers, sucking his tongue into her mouth while continuing to thrust her hips, letting him know the sex had just begun. They ended up going from the couch to the floor and from the floor to the tub. When they were finally done, they cuddled on the couch to smoke a blunt and bask in the afterglow of good sex.

"I want to be your queen," Larena confessed while staring deep into his eyes.

Junior knew this moment would come. And although he felt a connection to Larena, he wasn't ready to make her his queen. Yet.

Larena saw his indecision. "You don't have to make a decision right now. You don't have to rush. I'm not going anywhere. I just wanted you to know how I feel."

Instead of speaking, he gave her a reassuring kiss. And that's when his phone rang. It was a text from Six. He was in the city. "Hey, Six just sent me a text. I need to go meet with him."

Disappointment flashed in her green eyes, but it was gone just as fast. "Go do your thing. Tell Six I said hi."

***

Junior pulled up to the hood and saw a small gathering in front of his mother's house. Six, Santana, John, T-Murda, and RIP stood around smoking and talking.

"The boss of all bosses!" Junior grinned as he hugged Six. "What's good, big bro?"

"I'm good, boss. How you doing?"

"I'm alive and free, so I can't complain."

"Complaining won't solve nothing anyway," Santana said.

Junior looked at the brown-skinned warrior woman standing next to his brother and smiled. "I'm glad to see that my brother took my advice and kept you close."

She gave a cocky smirk. "When God blesses you with a virtuous woman, you better recognize it."

Her words made a vision of Larena flash in Junior's mind as he turned to his brother.

"She know scripture and she can fight. When y'all getting married?" John asked.

"Only God knows the future, my nigga," Six laughed. "But I need you to take a ride with me, Junior. We need to talk about your future."

Junior looked to his Grind Squad niggas. "When I get back, y'all already know what it is!"

"Chopping bricks like karate!" T-Murda rapped.

"You already know!" Junior said before following Six to the Audi A8 parked at the curb. Santana walked around to the driver's seat while the brothers climbed in the backseat.

"Before we talk business, I wanna talk to you about Nicole," Six said, giving his little brother a serious look. "You fumbled the ball at the one-yard line, my nigga."

"C'mon, brah. Wasn't no way I could be in two places at the same time. Nicole lied to Mama. She went out there and did some bullshit and got fucked up."

Six stared at Junior for a moment. "If Mooka grow up and fall off into some bullshit and get jammed up, is it his fault for getting in trouble or your fault for not equipping him with the skills to get through the pitfalls of life?"

Junior thought about the question. The easy way out was to blame Mooka for making a bad decision. But if a father doesn't equip his children to succeed, the father is to blame just as much as the child.

"The father is to blame."

"None of us, except Renae, had a daddy growing up. Mama was our mama and daddy. She did what she could, but it was some things she couldn't teach us. Some shit we had to learn on our own. The point of our lessons wasn't for us. I learned lessons and taught them to you. You was supposed to follow my example and pass down what you learned. When I told you to take care of the family, that's what I meant. Teach them and show them the way. You right, Nicole made a bad decision, but you are partly responsible for her bad decision."

"I never thought about it like that," Junior responded thoughtfully.

"I know. And I'm responsible for that. I should have better equipped you. We both gotta turn Nicole's L into a lesson. We gotta do a better job making sure the family good. You feel me?"

Junior nodded. "Yeah. We gotta do better."

"Ain't nothing we can do now. I got her a lawyer. They charging her as a juvenile, which is good. The most time she can get is five years. Bad thing is, she can't get bail, so she gotta sit in there and wait to see what happens."

"Least they not charging her as an adult. Armed robbery is forty years."

Six nodded before extending a hand. They shook. Everything was good with the brothers again.

"So, how is life? What's going on with you?"

Junior shook his head. " Man, it's too much. Way too fucking much. But I'm figuring it out. I just need to make this move and get to the next level. Once I do that, everything will work itself out."

"You know that's not how it works, right? Shit don't just figure itself out because you got more money. More money brings more problems. Puffy was right."

Junior let out a long breath. "Man, Quitta found out I was fucking with Larena, and I think she called the police on me."

Six lifted an eyebrow. "You talking about Patricia's friend Larena from back in the day?"

Junior nodded. "I just left her right before I came back to the hood."

"You think Quitta called the police on you for fucking with her and you still fucking with her?"

"It ain't that easy. I'm not fucking with Quitta no more. I'm staying with Mama for right now. I can't be with nobody that calls the police. That shit was vindictive as hell. Ain't no telling what else she would do to spite me."

"But you knew that after she fucked Lo-Dog."

"Yeah, well I'm not about to let this one go. I'm good. Plus, the same detective that knocked Nicole try'na knock me for the body in Lacrosse. Somebody up there talking. The nigga came to the interrogation room and told me he try'na fry my ass."

Six's eyes grew wide. "What the fuck, Junior!? That's some serious shit, nigga!"

"I know. And I still gotta deal with this Fredo situation with Quitta. Like I said, shit is too much."

"You know money ain't gon' help none of the problems you just told me about, right? I think you need to fall back from everything. Lay low for a while. Right now might not be the right time to bring you in. You got alotta shit going on, my nigga."

"C'mon, brah! Don't do me like that," Junior said, on the verge of begging. "You know how hard I been busting my ass to get this seat at the table? Shit, that's the reason me and Quitta broke up because I was grinding too hard. She went through my phone because she thought I was cheating because I was staying out too late. Don't let the stress and shit I went through be for nothing, my nigga. I worked hard for this spot."

Six stared into his little brother's eyes, judging him. Junior was involved in way too much shit. The Folks had a hit out on him, the police were looking for him for a body in Lacrosse, and the Milwaukee Police were looking for his baby mama for another homicide. But he did grind up the money and put his relationship on the line for a seat at the table.

"What the fuck, Junior?" Six breathed, shaking his head. "You putting me in a fucked-up spot. If you wasn't my brother, I woulda been washed my hands and probably sent a team to get rid of you. You got so much shit going on, and that shit could easily trickle upstream. I don't know what to do. This not an easy decision."

"Brah, give me a chance to show you that I can handle this. All the shit that I'm dealing with started before you offered me the seat. Besides Quitta calling the police. Since then, all I been doing is hustling. They was still investigating me in Lacrosse, but I just didn't know. Shit, Quitta calling the police helped me find out that mu'fuckas up north was talking. I got plans for taking Parklawn and I'mma figure out a way to address that shit in Lacrosse. Gimmie a shot, brah. I'm ready."

Six continued to evaluate his brother. Then a slight smile cracked his lips. "You better get yo' shit together, Junior. I'm not bullshitting. The niggas that I fuck with don't play. They will not hesitate to kill you, and it won't be shit that I can do about it."

"I got it, brah. That's my word. I can do this. I'm ready."

"Okay. Where is the money?"

"It's at my apartment on Green Tree."

Santana followed Junior's directions and parked outside the apartment while he went to get the money.

"What you think, baby? Did I make the right decision?" Six asked, second-guessing his decision to bring Junior in.

Santana met his eyes in the rear-view mirror. "Sometimes we can be blinded by our love. Your little brother is a real hot boy. If he was a stranger, I would have told you to kill him. But he's also a hustler. And he's your little brother. You can't turn your back on him now."

Six understood what she said and the things she didn't say. Only time would tell if he made the right decision.

"Call the pilots and tell them we on the way."

Junior came back outside a few moments later with the money in a Louis Vuitton bag. "When do I get to meet the plug?" he asked as he slid into the backseat.

"We going to Tennessee to see him," Six said as he checked the time on his Cartier watch. "We should be there in about two hours."

Junior looked confused. "We driving all the way to Tennessee in two hours?"

Six and Santana laughed. "Nah, nigga. We flying. Private."

Junior looked even more confused. "Private? Like, in a private plane?"

Six looked in his little brother's eyes intently. "My nigga, tonight you about to see a lot of shit that you probably never imagined you would see. The only thing I'mma tell you is to act like this shit ain't nothing to you and don't embarrass me. A'ight?"

Santana drove the Audi to a private airfield near Mitchell International Airport. After showing a membership badge to security, she drove inside the private airport and past rows of airplane hangars. Junior looked around in amazement as the Audi stopped in front of a white-and-blue-striped Lear 60xR seven-passenger private jet.

"On what, we finna fly in a private jet, my nigga!? On what?" Junior asked, excitement dancing in his eyes.

"This is how real bosses move. Remember what I told you," Six said calmly. "Act like this shit ain't nothing."

They hopped out of the Audi and climbed the steps of the mid-sized jet. After they were buckled in, the pilot taxied the runway before putting the jet in the air. Two hours later, they landed on an airstrip at a private airport in Tennessee where a driver waited in a white Rolls Royce Dawn. From the airport they were driven to the Hampton Reserve, a gated community in Brentwood, Tennessee. After driving past several sprawling million-dollar mansions, the Rolls pulled into the driveway of a 1.6-acre cul-de-sac lot of the Morning Glory Courte Estate. After being checked by a security team, the driver parked the Rolls Royce near a fleet of luxury cars.

Junior climbed from the Rolls and stared at the cars in amazement. For him, looking at the red Ferrari 488 Spider, blue Lamborghini Urus, and silver Bentley Bentayga was like walking past space-ships. They followed a tall and muscular nigga in a black suit into the grand entry hall of the mansion and into a formal living area with floor-to-ceiling windows. People dressed in clothes that didn't come out until next year were gathered around a short, clean-shaved Asian man. He was telling a story and the people around him looked like they were eating the words as they left his mouth. His eyes ran across Six, Santana, and Junior quickly as he spoke.

"So the guy gives me some bullshit story about how he had to pay the government five million in back taxes so he wasn't able to cover our agreement. I told him that I didn't give a shit because I had to give the government ten million. When he saw that excuse didn't work, he starts playing some little ass violin while telling me about the ex-wife that cleaned him out and the mistress with expensive habits. Right then, I knew he wasn't going to be able to cover his end of the agreement, so I offered him a deal he couldn't refuse. Now I own the rights to every movie produced by Hawkvision Studios for the next five years. And that new deal is worth five times what the original agreement was. I swear, I can't make this stuff up. Smart people are stupid."

The people that had been listening to the story laughed like the Asian man was Dave Chapelle.

"Now, excuse me for a moment. I need to speak with my friend," he said before walking over to the newcomers. "James! Welcome back, my brother!" he grinned, greeting Six by his real name.

"Glad to be back." Six nodded. "I told you I had someone for you to meet. This is my little brother, Junior. Junior, this is Mr. Chow."

The Asian man smiled with his lips, but his eyes were hard and serious. "I heard that you are going to take over a project."

Junior nodded. "Aim for the moon. If I miss, I'll still be among the stars."

Mr. Chow laughed. "No, my friend. The projects are nowhere near the stars or the moon. That is more like the first level of space. Aiming for that moon is taking over this entire state. Come with me," he said, wrapping an arm around Junior's shoulder. "We have a lot to discuss."

They walked through the mansion and out onto the patio. On the other side of the estate was another mansion with a resort type atmosphere. There was a pool with a waterfall, slide, and swim-up bar. Bad ass women were lounging around the pool area drinking. When Mr. Chow walked by, a lot of the women tried to get him to play in the water. After declining, he led the way into the mansion. The family room had been modeled after a casino. There was a large table in the middle of the room where six men were playing poker. The room also held a fireplace, sitting area, and bar. Women served drinks and provided entertainment.

"About time you left those schmucks and joined the real party," a heavy-set white man with an East Coast accent teased Mr. Chow.

"What's up, James? Who's the Boy Scout?" an older dark-skinned man asked, eyeing Junior.

Six sat down at the table and motioned for Junior to sit next to him. "What up, fellas? Let me introduce y'all to my little brother, Junior. Junior, this is The Family. You already met Mr. Chow. This is David East, Brian Tammany, Steven Denny, Bradley Fresno, Christian Stone, and Gerald Housman."

"Junior wants to take over the projects," Mr. Chow teased.

Brian Tammany, a tall, well-built, biracial man laughed loudly. "Let me guess? You also want to clean your dirty money with a record label that you created in your mother's basement? And spend all of your money on jewelry and cars?"

Junior was caught off guard by their demeaning comments and taunts. He looked to Six for a sign on how to respond. Six stared in his eyes intently, excited to see how his little brother would deal with the new situation. Junior turned his attention to Brian Tammany, smiling with his lips while his stare remained serious. "The projects taught me that a bad move will leave you dead, broke, in jail, or fucked up. A key to success is being able to assess new situations and make the necessary adjustments. You heard projects and turned me into a stereotype and counted me out. The good thing about being counted out is you'll never see you coming."

Brian Tammany's smile disappeared. "You think some wise words will get you success? It takes more than that to reach this level. Why are you here? What do you want?"

"I'm here because I'm ready. And as far as what I want," Junior paused and looked at all of the rich nigga amenities around the room. "I want everything that this life has to offer."

Six smiled proudly.

Chapter 8

Two weeks later

Dazè walked down the lower tier for the final time, throwing up the pitch forks to his niggas as they wished him well from their cells.

"Get out there and have yo' way, Zè. The world needs more real niggas!" Big Snake called.

"I'mma do it for all my niggas! Love, boy!"

"Make sure you stay away from them ops and suckas!" Chip yelled.

"I'm allergic to suckas and all my ops ain't breathing no more!" Dazè laughed.

"Geez, Crawford. You act like you don't want to leave," Sergeant Wicket yelled, waiting at the end of their tier.

"You know I gotta show love to all my niggas, Sarge. I'mma legend in The Bay. This mu'fucka ain't gon' be the same without me."

"You can say that shit again. The less riots and bleeding bodies that we see makes my job easier."

Dazè and the sergeant shared a knowing look. "I don't know what you talking about, Sarge. I'm a humble man."

The correctional officer laughed. "Yeah. And my dick is twelve inches long. Let's get you the hell out of here."

The sergeant led Dazè through the prison and up front where inmates were processed in and out of the prison. Two white shirts, Captain Sanders and Lieutenant Gorbach, along with Green Bay's Warden, Michael Mushers, were all waiting.

"I get the whole Klan, huh?" Dazè smiled, loving this moment. He waited thirteen years to see the faces of his haters as he was leaving.

"You made it. Congratulations, Mr. Crawford." The warden smiled, extending a hand.

Dazè looked at the outstretched hand before mugging the shit out of the warden. "Save yo' congratulations, man. If it was up to you, I'd still be in the hole on AC. You know you hate to see me leave. Fuck you, chump."

The warden's eyes grew wide with anger, and his face flushed red.

"That ain't necessary, Crawford," Lieutenant Gorbach spoke up. "We came with good tidings."

"Man, fuck all of y'all and y'all good tidings. Where the fuck was that shit at when y'all was locking us down and beating our ass? I don't wanna hear that shit. Gimmie my clothes so I can get the fuck outta here."

Captain Sanders tossed him a shopping bag. "I'm not going to be professional or kiss your ass, Crawford. I'm going to keep a cell open for you because I know you'll be back. You're a gangster, and gangsters end up two places. Dead or in a cell."

Dazè laughed at the captain's words. "That's the realest shit you ever said. And fuck you, too. Where do I change at?"

The warden pointed to a holding cell. "Just for you. It'll be here when you get back."

"I bet all y'all praying for me to lose," Dazè said as he stepped into the cell and began changing out of the prison greens. "But what y'all don't realize is that I need y'all prayers. I need y'all hate. I used that as my motivation to make it through y'all bitch ass system. And I'mma keep using it to win. Y'all keep praying on my down-fall. Thank you."

After changing into a Ralph Lauren fit and a pair of white Air Force Ones, Dazè checked his reflection in the small stainless-steel mirror above the toilet-sink combo. Six crispy cornrows to the back. Freshly trimmed beard and mustache. His peanut butter complexion shined like new money. He wouldn't call himself a pretty boy, but he definitely knew he was handsome. And the lean muscles packed onto his 6'2", 195-pound frame was the icing on the cake. He stepped from the cell feeling like new money.

The warden walked up with a face card and release papers. "Tell me your name, date of birth, and DOC number."

"Dazè Crawford, 10-26-94, 547389."

The warden handed him the release papers. "Your boxes are waiting outside. And I'll keep a cell for you."

Dazè sneered before grabbing his papers and walking toward the exit. On the outside he was cool and calm but inside, he was jumping up and down like a kid that was going to Disney World. He had finally made it. Thirteen long ass years of incarceration were a few steps away from being over. The correctional staff followed a few steps behind. When they came to the door, Dazè stepped outside and squinted at the bright sun. He paused, closing his eyes to soak in the sun. It was finally over.

"Dazè! Hey, Dazè!"

He opened his eyes and saw his little sister, Serena, standing outside the 15-foot iron gate, jumping up and down excitedly. His other sister, Tamar, was recording his release on her phone. His mother and grandmother were standing next to his sisters, smiling like they won a prize.

"Y'all gon' help me with my boxes?" he asked the white shirts as he grabbed a box.

The white shirts reluctantly bent down to grab boxes as the warden led the way to the final gate.

"Good morning, family. You can have your loved one back." The warden smiled while unlocking the gate. "Take care of yourself, Mr. Crawford."

Dazè ignored the warden as he was mobbed by the women. After shouts, screams, and kisses, he packed his boxes in the back of the Blazer before climbing in the backseat with his sisters.

"You finally made it out, Dazè. What you wanna do first?" his grandmother asked from the passenger seat.

"I want some real food! Stop at the nearest restaurant so I can eat!"

The nearest restaurant was a McDonald's. Dazè ordered four Big Macs, a ten-piece Chicken McNugget, and a Sprite to wash it all down. The fast food was so good that he moaned during the first couple of bites.

"Damn, Dazè!" Tamar frowned. "It sound like you and yo' food need to get a room."

"If you seen what I been eating for the last thirteen years, you would be moaning, too."

After a two-hour ride, Dazè spotted the green highway sign that told him they were entering Milwaukee. He looked around anxiously, not wanting to miss a thing as they rode through the city. He found it strange how everything looked the same and different. When the Blazer turned onto 47th Street, Dazè smiled as he got his first glimpse of Parklawn since 2009. Nostalgia gripped him as he remembered running through the projects raising hell. About twenty-five people were gathered in front of his grandmother's apartment. When he climbed from the truck, he was mobbed by friends and loved ones.

"Welcome home, Dazè!"

He shook hands, hugged, and kissed everybody while locking eyes with a brown-skinned woman with dimples.

"Dazè, what it do, nigga!?" Junior smiled while hugging the newly freed man. "Damn, you got big as hell!"

"Junior, what's good, nigga? You look like you eating good," Dazè commented while checking out the iced-out watch on his arm.

"After you finish with the family, come find me. I got something for you."

"Fa sho." Dazè nodded before turning to John. He looked up at him with surprise. "Damn, nigga! On what, you like six foot five, John."

"Six-six, nigga. Gimmie all mine. Welcome home, my nigga." John grinned as the men hugged.

"Hell yeah. I'm back, my nigga," Dazè said before getting to the woman with the dimples.

She wore a red and black Adidas T-shirt, black jeans, and red and black Adidas trainers. "Welcome home, Dazè," she said, showing a pretty smile.

"Good looking. Do I know you?"

She smiled sweetly, hitting him with the dimples again. "Not really. I was young when you left. I'm Renae, Junior's sister."

Dazè thought for a moment, then his eyes popped. "I remember you. Lil' Renae. Shit. You all grown now, huh?"

"Yeah. I'm twenty-five and loving life." She smiled while checking out Dazè. He had the sexy thug look on lock. The Ralph Lauren shirt hugged his chest, biceps, and shoulders just right. Renae didn't know how, but she was going to make him her own.

"You still stay with Mom?" Dazè fished, nodding toward Gail's house.

"Yep. Still ain't left the nest yet. What about you? Where you staying?"

"I'm paroled at my grandmother house. I missed Parklawn. It don't look like nothing changed."

"Dazè, you gotta come here! Look at Mama and Granny dancing!" Serena yelled from the porch before running in the house.

"I gotta go see this. I'll see you around, right?" Dazè asked, holding eye contact as he backed away.

Renae hit him with the dimples again. "You can see me whenever you want."

Dazè went inside and kicked it with the family for a few hours, meeting cousins and other family members that had been born while he was locked up, and being reintroduced to family members that had gone from children to adulthood. When the novelty of his release had worn off and people started to leave, Dazè stepped onto the porch with Tamar.

"I'm so happy that you finally home, Dazè. It's good to almost have the family back together."

"Shit, I'm happy as hell to be here. When I first got locked up, some nights I didn't think I was gon' make it out. Now I'm here. When Big Dogg get out, then we'll all be together again. That's what I'm really looking forward to."

"So, what are you going to do? Go to school? Get a job? I know you not about to get in the streets, are you?"

"I'm thinking about school. A degree in business or something. I'm on parole so I gotta get a job, but I don't wanna work forever. I eventually wanna start my own business."

Tamar smiled. "That's what I'm talking about, bro. I like the way you thinking. Now you gotta find the right woman to help you along the way. Whatever woman you choose gotta get my approval, too. Can't bring any old body home."

Dazè looked toward Gail's house. "What's up with Renae?"

Tamar's eyes grew wide. "Ooh! You already got yo' eyes on Junior's little sister, huh? Renae is cool. I never really heard nothing bad about her. She might be good for you."

"You think so?" Dazè asked, thinking about her dimples.

Tamar nodded. "I do. Plus, I know her already so I don't gotta do too much digging. And, if she get on some bullshit, she live right across the street, and I can easily reach out and touch her."

***

"That nigga Dazè got big as hell," John commented as he and Junior walked through the projects.

"Yeah, he did. I can't believe that nigga did all that time. Thirteen years! That shit don't even seem possible," Junior said, unable to comprehend spending all that time locked up.

"That nigga big time insto, on what?" John cracked.

"Shit, he gotta be. Thirteen years will make anybody crazy," Junior said as he walked up on the porch of T-Murda's new spot and rang the doorbell.

"Who dat?" T-Murda called from inside.

"Junior."

When the door opened, T-Murda was smiling and showing every gold tooth in his mouth. "What up, cousin?"

"Shit. You got it. What's the word on that work?" Junior asked as he and John stepped inside.

"On my mama, the back door ain't stopped rocking all day. These mu'fuckas loving this shit, you hear me! Dope fiend parties all night long!"

Junior smiled at the report. Things were looking good. The first shipment from The Family dropped three days ago. Ten kilos of 85 percent pure cocaine. He bussed down each kilo with 2,000 grams of baking soda, turning the ten kilos into thirty. And according to

T-Murda, it was still good dope. The Parklawn Grind Squad was about to be rich!

"Damn, we about to be eating, my nigga. You hear me? We about to be eating!" Junior celebrated.

"What they say about the other shit? We need to sew up everything. Weed and pills," T-Murda said.

"I gotta prove that I can handle this first shipment. These real live made niggas. Once I take back that 250, then I'mma speak on the other shit," Junior explained. "I'm finna go holla at RIP. Is you coming to Sammy D party tonight?"

"I don't know, my nigga. This paper got a nigga chasing," he said before going to the closet and grabbing a Burberry satchel. He pulled out a handful of money. "The day ain't even over with and I already made five stickers! I'm try'na see if I can do ten!"

Junior loved his cousin's grind. "That's what I'm talking 'bout, cuz. Run it up!"

After leaving T-Murda, the brothers headed toward RIP's trap when they saw Dazè standing on his grandmother's porch. "Dazè, what you on, fool?" Junior asked.

Dazè smiled, riding a natural high. "I'm just staring at freedom, my nigga. I ain't on shit."

Junior and John shared a look, both men remembering their conversation about Dazè being institutionalized.

"Come fuck with us for a minute," John said. "We just making some rounds. You want something to smoke?"

Dazè's eyes grew wide as he leapt from the porch. "What kinda question is that, nigga? I been smoking penitentiary joints and one hitters for thirteen years. Where that good shit at?"

"You don't know nothing about smoking out of an apple," Junior laughed as he pulled out a sack and a wrap.

"Nigga, I think I'm the one that invented smoking out of an apple," Dazè cracked as he rolled up the blunt.

"So, what you on, my nigga? You try'na get this paper?" John asked.

"Fam, I told Granny n'em that I was gon' work and go to school. But on some real shit, I can't see myself punching no clocks and taking exams. After everything that I been through, working a nine to five is the last thing on my mind. I need some real paper."

Junior nodded. "I feel you. I felt the same way when I did my bid. I wanted to do the right thing. But then I got hit with an offer I couldn't refuse. Been in the streets ever since. But now niggas on another level. Whenever you ready, just let me know. Matter of fact, I got something to show you."

Junior led the way into RIP's trap and made the introduction.

"RIP, this Tamar brother, Dazè. He just got out today. Dazè, this my cousin, RIP."

"What's good, family?" RIP nodded as they shook hands.

"I'm loving my freedom and this good ass weed." Dazè grinned, high as hell.

"Shit, let me hit that shit. How long you do?" RIP asked, reaching for the blunt

"Thirteen long ass years."

RIP choked on the weed and looked at Dazè like he was an alien. "Thirteen years!? On what?"

Junior laughed at RIP's reaction. "Real shit. Nigga a muthafuckin' souljah."

"Damn, my nigga. You had some pussy yet? I bet you gon' break a bitch in half!" RIP laughed.

"Or fall in love," John cracked. "Nigga dick tender as a muthafucka. Soon as he stick it in, he gon' buss a nut and fall in love." Everybody burst out laughing.

"Y'all niggas clowning," Dazè laughed. "But nah, I ain't hit nothing yet. I been fucking with the family all day. My little white bitch supposed to be pulling up later tonight though."

"She nice?" John asked.

Dazè shrugged. "When a nigga doing a long bid, you don't give a fuck what a bitch look like. Long as she sending them money orders, that's all that matter."

"Talk that pimp shit!" John cheered, stomping his feet.

"Nah, my nigga. Fuck that. We finna get you some pussy right now," Junior said, pulling out his phone. "Aye, John, what's the one lil' vibe over 45th and Hope name? Light skinned with the fatty. Tats on her face."

"Oh, you talking 'bout Lisa."

"Yeah, Lisa. And she active right now. I'm on her for you, my nigga. And she cold with the top."

John nodded. "College degree with the head."

Dazè just smiled.

When Junior was live with her, he shared the phone with Dazè. She was a light-skinned cutie with big lips and dollar sign tattoos above both eyebrows. "Aye, Lisa! what you on, baby?"

"Hey, Junior! What's good, my nigga? You know a bitch out here try'na run up a check. You try'na touch my tonsils or what, nigga?"

"Listen, my nigga need to see you. We over on 46th and Congress. Slide through and I got you."

She smiled and licked out her tongue. "Okay, baby. Ooh, and you cute, too. Wait 'til you see my pussy, baby. This bitch is beautiful!"

"What the fuck was that?" Dazè asked after Junior hung up the phone.

"That's Lisa, my nigga. She wild. Real life sack chaser. And she gon' get you right. You with us for the rest of the day. My nigga Sammy D throwing a party at Birdie's tonight and you with us. RIP, how much money you got?"

"Shit, I did like thirty-five so far."

"Give it to Dazè," Junior said before going in his pocket and matching RIP's thirty-five hundred. "Welcome home, boss."

Lisa messaged Junior a few minutes later to let him know she was outside. All the men ogled her body when she stepped inside the apartment wearing a sexy white athletic suit that barely covered her big ass titties and showed her camel toe.

"Damn, baby. You wearing the fuck out them leggings," Junior said while palming her ass.

"Look at y'all niggas in here looking like money," she said while licking her lips and grabbing Junior's crotch. "I'll let y'all run a train on me right now for five blues. What's up?"

The men looked tempted to take her up on the offer, but Junior shut it down. "We good. This my nigga, Dazè. He just came home from doing a bid. Bless my nigga."

Lisa's eyes lit up as she slid over to Dazè and began feeling on his body. "Damn, baby. You got muscles like Roman Reigns. How long you do?"

Dazè palmed her ass while feeling up her body, his dick feeling like it was about to bust through his pants. "I just did thirteen years. Damn, you thick as fuck."

Lisa jumped back like Dazè pulled a gun. Hearing how much time he'd done spooked her. "Hold on, nigga! You ain't finna kill me!"

Everybody laughed.

"Stop playing and bless my nigga before he get blue balls," John cracked.

Lisa eased back over to Dazè. "Oh, my god. I'm a little scared for real. Don't break me, nigga."

"You good," Dazè laughed before nodding to RIP. "Can I use a room?"

"Mi casa, su casa."

Lisa led the way upstairs. Dazè followed her bouncing ass all the way to the room. As soon as the door closed, Lisa threw her purse on the dresser and began stripping.

"I charge by the nut. Fifty for some head. A blue face for some pussy or some ass."

Dazè mugged her when she mentioned ass. "Bitch, you think I'mma gump!?"

She looked apologetic. "I didn't mean it like that. Some niggas wanna fuck me in my ass."

Dazè continued to mug her as he got undressed. "I feel like you tried me, but I'mma let it slide. But just so you know, this big ass six-point star on my chest mean I'mma gangsta. I don't sit my G to the side for nothing."

"I really didn't mean no disrespect," she said, a little scared and turned on by his aggression. "I love gangstas."

Dazè stepped out of his boxers and pants, his dick pointing to the ceiling. "Show a real nigga some love then."

Lisa hit her knees and shoved his dick in her mouth like she was trying to swallow it. She went halfway down three or four times before his body went stiff.

"Awe, shit!" Dazè moaned as he began busting.

Lisa kept him in her mouth while jacking him off, waiting for him to finish so she could spit. Dazè kept on nutting, filling her mouth until nut was drizzling down her chin. When Lisa's mouth couldn't hold any more, she finally spit. Semen splashed on the floor like she threw up. She looked from the floor and up at Dazè in amazement as she wiped her mouth.

"Oh, my god! I never seen a nigga nut that much! What the fuck!?"

Dazè breathed hard like he ran a race. "Shit, I didn't even know I could nut that much. But I ain't done yet. What up with that pretty pussy?"

Lisa grabbed her purse and threw a box of condoms on the bed. "You probably gonna need all of them."

***

Dazè ended up spending five hundred dollars on Lisa in less than thirty minutes. Every time he stuck his dick in her pussy, he bust a nut. When he got to five, he let her leave before she dug too deep into his pocket. After spending the best five hundred dollars he ever spent, he rode with John and Junior to the mall. He got dripped in Versace before they went to see Gino the jeweler. Junior spent 10,000 icing up Dazè with a Cuban link and Jesus piece.

Later that night, they were in Birdie's kicking it like bosses. Sammy D rented out the club for his birthday, so it was a Parklawn gangsta party.

"On God, the bitch said the nigga bust so much nut that it could'da filled up this glass!" Junior laughed, holding up his drink. Everyone around him burst out laughing.

"Shit, what the fuck you thought, nigga?" Mike laughed. "That bitch lucky my nigga ain't kill her mu'fuckin' ass!"

"Thirteen years would have a nigga shit shooting like a water hose!" Fifty added.

There was another round of laughter.

"Aye, y'all niggas better hope y'all don't go through what I went through," Dazè chuckled, loving the vibe with his niggas. "I went in as a shorty, so I had to fight damn near every day to show them niggas I wasn't sweet. Knocking big niggas out. Niggas that was two or three times bigger than me."

"You a demon, my nigga!" Sammy D grinned, loving hearing about the violence. He lifted the bottle of Ace of Spades he was holding in the air and got everybody's attention. "Aye, y'all! Check it out! This nigga, Dazè, is a real-life demon! A muthafuckin' soulja that put in work and did his time and didn't snitch! Twenty-one gun salute to all the real niggas!"

Junior was saluting Dazè when he felt like somebody was watching him. He looked around the club until he locked eyes with a chubby dark-skinned nigga with blue dreads. The nigga looked away immediately. Junior knew the face, but he couldn't place it. He was about to ask Fifty about the nigga when John got his attention.

"Aye, look, brah," John said, pointing toward the bar.

Junior looked toward the bar and for a moment, he thought he was tripping. "What the fuck!?"

John looked stressed. "I can't believe Renae brought this bitch to the bar! Damn! Just fucked up my night."

Renae was at the bar with Nikki and Quitta. When Junior saw his baby mama, he got pissed off.

"Damn, my nigga. Both y'all bitches here," Black laughed.

"Ain't neither one of y'all getting some new pussy tonight," Toe Tagga cracked. "That's more pussy for me and you, Black!"

Junior left the VIP and stormed over to the women. "What the fuck you doing here?!"

Quitta looked at him from head to toe, amusement dancing in her eyes. "I'm out with my girls. What you mean? I'm grown."

"And she with me, nigga! She my sister," Renae said.

"We came out to have a good time, Junior. Don't kill our vibe," Nikki added.

Junior mugged all of their women, his stare lingering on Quitta.

"I must look good, huh? That's why you staring?" she asked, dancing to the music and teasing him.

Even though Junior was pissed off that she was in the club, he admitted that his baby mama looked good. Her hair was dyed emerald blue, her makeup was on point, and her body was going crazy in the little ass metallic dress that barely came to her thighs. "You a'ight. But y'all ain't coming in the VIP and blowing my nigga party. Where Mooka?"

"With my sister." Quitta rolled her eyes. "Gone back up in VIP and leave me alone. Ain't nobody gon' wanna talk to me with you hovering over me. Bye."

Junior had a vision of grabbing her by the hair and dragging her out of the club. But it was his nigga's birthday and they had plenty of bottles and bad bitches in the VIP.

"A'ight, Quitta." He smiled. "Do yo' thang and I'mma do mine."

Quitta's smile matched his. "Peace."

Junior went back to the VIP and tried to enjoy the party, but he couldn't. Quitta showed up and fucked off his night. He hadn't been around her much since moving out. The only time they saw each other was when she dropped off Mooka by his mom's house or picked up some money. Their words were few. Hi, bye, and how Mooka was doing. But tonight, the only thing he was concerned about was what nigga she was talking to or dancing with.

Jealousy burned in his chest as he watched her on the dance-floor. He grabbed a random female and danced with her, grinding on her ass while feeling her body. When Quitta saw him dancing with the woman, she pushed her ass on the nigga she was dancing with and started twerking. She and the stranger looked like they were fucking. The nigga got geeked and started grabbing all over her ass and titties. When Quitta realized the nigga was doing too much, she tried to push him away. The drinks wouldn't allow the nigga to take the hint. Instead, he got more aggressive.

Renae and Nikki were dancing close by and when they saw the nigga doing too much, they rushed over to help their girl. The nigga was too horny and turned up to be stopped. He pushed Renae to the side and damn near snatched Quitta's dress off. Junior grabbed a bottle of Ace and leapt the VIP rope, carrying the bottle like it was a sword. Dazè had been watching Renae and peeped everything. Without being told, he grabbed two Hennessey bottles and followed close behind Junior, ready to smash the nigga that pushed Renae. Junior walked up to the nigga that had been grabbing Quitta without saying a word. He lifted the bottle and let it do the talking. He smashed the nigga in the head several times, knocking him out on the dancefloor. When his niggas tried to rush, Dazè started swinging the Hennessey bottles, busting niggas upside the head.

"Hey! Stop! Break that shit up!" security called, rushing over and grabbing Junior and Dazè.

"Let me go, bitch ass nigga!" Junior yelled, struggling to free himself from the bouncer's grasp. "Let me go!"

"Nah, nigga! You gotta get the fuck outta here!" he said, carrying Junior to the door.

The other bouncer was doing the same thing to Dazè. The manager was shooing Renae, Nikki, and Quitta toward the door.

"We didn't do shit!" Nikki complained.

"Y'all didn't see that bitch ass nigga just damn near try to rape me!?" Quitta yelled.

"I'll blow this muthafucka up if you touch me, bitch ass nigga!" Renae threatened, shoving the manager.

"Get the fuck outta here right now or I'm calling the police. All y'all gotta go, right now!"

When they were thrown out, Junior shoved Quitta against the wall angrily. "This why the fuck I told yo' ass to leave, bitch. Look what the fuck you just did! If I wasn't there, that nigga would have fucked you up!"

"Fuck you, Junior. You the one in there dancing on them bitches. I can do whatever I want."

Junior pushed her onto the building again. "You stupid as fuck! In there acting like a hoe. I should beat yo' ass."

Renae pushed Junior away from Quitta. "Leave her alone, nigga! It ain't her fault that nigga was crazy. Fuck wrong with you?!"

Junior was about to rush Renae when Dazè stepped in front of him. "Chill, fam! Chill!"

Junior huffed and puffed angrily, wanting to beat Renae and Quitta's ass.

"What the fuck just happened?" Sammy D asked as he and some of their niggas came outside.

Junior pointed at Quitta. "This bitch got us kicked out. I'm finna bounce, fam."

"What happened? What y'all beat them niggas ass?" Toe Tagga asked.

"Nigga damn near tried to rape Quitta," Renae explained. "Now Junior try'na make it seem like it's her fault."

"It is her fault, nigga! And yours too!" Junior snapped. "If y'all wouldn'ta brought y'all stupid asses in here thinking y'all on something and try'na be some hoes, that shit wouldn't have happened."

Renae tried to swing at Junior. "Call me another hoe and we boxing, nigga!"

Junior tried to get at his sister, but Toe Tagga and Sammy D grabbed him.

Dazè grabbed Renae around the waist and held her. "C'mon, Renae. Where you parked at? Let me take you to yo' car."

"Aye, Junior, go home, nigga. Leave yo' sister alone and go home," Sammy D laughed.

"C'mon, baby daddy. Take me home. Let's go," Quitta said, grabbing his arm.

Junior snatched away from Quitta. "Let me go, nigga," he snapped, storming away.

"Junior, I'mma catch a ride with sis," Dazè called.

Junior acknowledged him with a wave of the hand and kept walking. Quitta took off her heels to keep up with him. They hopped in the Lexus truck without a word and rode in silence. About five minutes into the ride, Quitta dropped the bomb.

"I'm two months pregnant."

Junior mugged her for a long time before shaking his head.

Chapter 9

When Junior opened his eyes, he remembered where he saw the nigga that was watching him at the club last night. He was BGM. One of Fredo's niggas. He was in the club the night Quitta set him up. And now he knew who Junior was.

"Fuck," he cursed, reaching for his phone to check the time.

It was 8:47 a.m. He sent Fifty a text, letting him know to holla when he woke up. Then he dropped the phone and let his thoughts roam. The shit with BGM was about to get serious. Everybody in the club knew the niggas in the VIP were from Parklawn. The BGM niggas were coming. He knew it. On top of that, Quitta claimed she was pregnant again. The timing couldn't have been worse. The police were still looking for her. He didn't even want to think about the new baby being born while Quitta was in jail. Plus, Fredo's niggas knew who they were. What if they moved while Quitta was dropping Mooka off at his mother's house?

Every way he looked at his situation, it looked bad. The only thing that was going in his favor was the hustle. The Family was going to increase the amount of product they shipped every time he made a payment. If things kept going the way they were going, he could be seeing M's in no time. The only thing that could thwart his plans was all of the drama. He needed to figure out a way to kill it. His success in the game was dependent on living long enough and being free long enough to get more work from The Family. The phone ringing grabbed his attention. It was Fifty.

"What's up, my nigga? You woke?"

"I just seen yo' text. What's good?" Fifty asked, his voice still scratchy.

"I seen one of them BGM niggas in the club last night. I meant to say something to you about it last night, but I got threw off by Quitta."

"On what? What he look like?"

"A black ass, chubby nigga with blue dreads. I felt the nigga watching me. When I looked at him, he looked away. I didn't realize he was BGM until I just woke up."

"That shit sound fucked up, brah. Damn. Now they know we from Parklawn. We gon' have to get on them niggas ass. I'm finna get up. I'mma meet you in the hood in a minute."

"Why you didn't tell me you seen one of them niggas in the club last night?"

Junior turned his head and saw Quitta staring at him, sleep still in her eyes.

"I didn't know it was a BGM nigga until just now. I caught the nigga watching me last night but I couldn't remember where I seen his face. Then y'all caused a distractions and I forgot about the nigga."

Quitta turned her head and stared at the ceiling. "Now they know who we is, huh?"

Junior shook his head. "Yep."

Quitta rolled over to face him again, fear in her eyes. "I think we should leave. Let's go back to Lacrosse. These niggas is gon' come for us. We gotta protect our kids."

Junior shook his head. "I can't leave. Not now. I just got the first batch in. I gotta get this money."

"You don't gotta be here. John n'em can hustle. Plus, you can get money in Lacrosse, too. You can spread the hustle and make more money."

Junior admitted that she had a point. "It ain't that easy, Quitta. I'm try'na take over Parklawn. I gotta oversee it. I wanna eventually spread out, but first I gotta lock down my projects. I can't leave."

Quitta got mad. "Nigga, you a daddy first. You gotta protect Mooka and the baby in my stomach. That's first and foremost. All that other shit come second. Our lives might be in danger, nigga. What the fuck don't you understand about that?"

Junior thought for a moment. "You go. Take Mooka. I'll bring y'all back when I figure everything out."

Quitta didn't like the option. "So, you want me to raise them by myself?"

"You got family up there. Plus, I'mma come when I can."

"No, Junior. I want you to come with me. I want us to be a family. I want you to be there when I have the baby. You missed Mooka being born and I don't want you to miss this one."

Junior became silent. Quitta wanted to be a family. He didn't. Their relationship had changed, but he didn't have the words to describe how it changed. But things were definitely different. He still loved her, but it was starting to fade. He didn't want to be with her, but he didn't want her to be with nobody else. Just thinking about it all made his head hurt. All he wanted to do was focus on getting money.

"What are you thinking about?" Quitta asked.

"I'm thinking about protecting you and the baby and Mooka. Y'all should leave."

Quitta searched his eyes, looking for what he wasn't saying. "You don't want to be a family no more?"

"We gon' always be family. We got kids."

"You know what I'm saying, Junior. I came to the club last night to get you back. To put our family back together. I feel like the new baby could be a new beginning for us. I still want to be with you. Last night you fucked me like I was still your girl. Am I still your girl?"

Junior let out a stressed breath and looked away. When he turned to look at Quitta again, there were tears in her eyes. She knew it was over. "Quitta, I'mma always love you. And I—"

"Get out my house, Junior."

"Wait. I'm try'na explain something to you."

Tears rolled down Quitta's cheeks, getting bigger and bigger. "I don't wanna hear that shit, nigga. Save yo' excuses and get the fuck outta my house. I don't need you. I can do bad all by my damn self."

***

Dazè ran his hands through Jeni's blonde hair as she worked her lips up and down his pole. He got up with her last night after leaving the club. He really wanted to spend the night with Renae, but he wasn't going to shit on Jeni. Not after she had spent the last seven years accepting his calls, writing him, and sending money orders. She showed loyalty, and he would honor her sacrifices by spending his first night of freedom with her. Now they were locked in a room at the Radisson, and she woke him up making love to him with her mouth.

"Get them balls, baby," Dazè groaned.

Jeni maintained eye contact as she began tonguing his balls. Dazè closed his eyes, loving the pleasure. And then his phone rang. He reached for it and checked the screen. It was Junior.

"What up, fam?" he answered.

"Shit. Seeing what's up with you. What you on?"

Dazè locked eyes with Jeni as she started sucking him again. "I'm at the telly with my snow bunny. What's up?"

"I got some shit I need to holla at you about. What time you coming back to Parklawn?"

"Uh, I probably be through there in a lil' while. Let me get back with shorty and I'mma hit you when I'm on my way."

"Okay. Get at me."

After hanging up the phone, Dazè focused all of his attention back on Jeni. A few minutes later, he was busting in her mouth. They got in another round of fucking before taking showers and getting dressed. While Dazè was putting on his shirt, Jeni watched him.

"Why you looking at me like that?" he asked.

"I'm still in shock that you're actually free and I got to spend the night with you. I can only imagine how you're feeling after sitting in prison for thirteen years."

Dazè sat next to her on the bed. "I'm not gonna even lie. When I opened my eyes in this hotel room, for a minute I thought I was dreaming. Then I looked over at you sleeping and knew it was real. I feel a little weird because maximum security was my normal life, and then all of a sudden I get threw back in the world and I'm free to do whatever I want. That sound insto, huh?"

146

"No. I think it sounds normal considering everything that you've been through. I'm surprised you can even sit still. I probably wouldn't be able to."

Dazè laughed. "You make crazy sound normal."

"Isn't everybody a little crazy?" she giggled. "I know I am."

They became quiet for a moment, staring into each other's eyes. Dazè was thinking about the real and genuine love she had shown him while he was locked up. Jeni was wondering if she would ever see him again. So she asked.

"Am I going to see you again?"

Dazè looked into her brown eyes. He loved her unconditionally. She was a rare and precious soul in a world full of selfish and greedy people. "Yeah, you will definitely see me again. I'mma call every day like I did while I was locked up. I told you that you my nigga for life. I meant that. You showed me love for seven years. Ain't no way I'mma get out here and forget about you. I love you for real. I'm gon' show you the same love that you showed me. If you ever need anything, just let me know and it's done."

The tender words made Jeni's insides melt. She leaned forward to kiss him. Dazè met her halfway.

"I wish you could be my boyfriend instead of Mike," she sighed. "Are you sure you don't want to give it a shot?"

Dazè laughed. "C'mon, Jeni. I never lied to you about nothing, so you know how I am. I got things to do. I gotta figure out what I like and what I want. I don't want to go there with you and end up hurting you and messing up our friendship. I want our bond to always be this strong."

Jeni's eye's reflected the love, respect, and admiration she had for Dazè. "Can't blame me for trying, right?" she giggled. "And you're right. We are great friends... With benefits," she added before leaning in for another kiss.

"A'ight. You gotta get back to Mike and I gotta holla at my nigga. I need you to drop me off."

After being dropped off in front of his grandmother's house, Dazè called Junior.

"What's good, Dazè? Where you at?"

"I'm stepping in Grams's house right now. Where you at?"

"I'm by my nigga Jeff house. Come holla at me when you come back out."

"Say less," Dazè said before hanging up. He stepped in the house to let his grandmother know he was okay and to see if she needed anything. When she told him she was good, he went to find Junior.

"Dazè, this my nigga, Jeff. He be letting us use his tip to buss moves. Jeff, this my nigga, Dazè," Junior introduced.

Dazè acknowledged the action with a nod. "Sup?"

"You got it, brah. Any nigga of Junior's is my nigga. Let me know if you need anything. Have a seat."

"Fa sho," Dazè agreed before sitting. "What you on, Junior? You and yo' baby mama figure that shit out last night?"

Junior shook his head. "Man, the shit got worse, my nigga. She pregnant."

Dazè looked at Jeff, wondering how Quitta being pregnant was worse. Jeff gave him the same look in return.

"I thought you would be happy that you about to have another shorty."

Junior shook his head again. "It's a lot of shit going on out here that you don't know nothing about. My BM helped me move on a nigga, and I had to whack him. A BGM nigga. The news got a picture of her saying she a person of interest. She ain't been identified yet. Plus, I got a body hanging over my head in Lacrosse. Somebody up there talking."

Dazè looked surprised. "Damn, nigga. You out here fucking it up. Fuck you was doing in Lacrosse?"

"G'tting' money. It was sweet up there and I was running it up. But niggas kept trying me. I end up burning this nigga from Chicago. The detective that booked my baby sister helping the police in Lacrosse. The nigga told me he was gon' cook me."

"Damn, family. That shit sound serious."

"On top of that, the Folks gotta green light on me. The nigga I whacked was a gangsta."

148

Disappointment flashed in Dazè's eyes. "You know I'mma gangsta, right?"

Junior nodded. "Yeah, I know. But you also my nigga. You not about to pick sides, is you?"

Dazè shook his head. "Nah. I don't know the nigga you got down on. Plus, we go back way too far. And you did more for me on my first day out than Folks did for me my whole life. But I can help you make it right. I got a slot and I'm on count in the city."

Junior's eyes popped. "On what?"

"On the G. I had Green Bay. That was my spot. I'mma call the city later and see if I can get that shit up off you."

Junior looked relieved. "Good looking, my nigga. Damn, I needed a win. You think you can help me with some more shit? Nigga, I got all types of problems," Junior cracked.

"I don't know, my nigga. You got a lot of shit going on."

"You ready for some more?"

Dazè's eye's grew wide. "You got some more shit?"

"Damn, Junior! When the fuck do you got time to get money with all this drama?" Jeff asked.

"All this shit was before the money. I'm try'na figure out a way to solve all this shit so I can focus on the money."

"So, what other shit you in?" Dazè asked.

"It was a BGM nigga in the club last night. I didn't realize who he was until this morning. I'm telling everybody so we can be on point when these niggas do come. You got a banger?"

"Nah, but I'mma need one. I'd rather be caught with it than without it."

"I'mma get that for you later. Now you see what I was saying about having another baby? I got too much shit going on."

Dazè nodded. "Yeah, you do got a lotta shit going on. But I also know that you know you gotta deal with that shit. Ain't no running. Life is a bitch, my nigga, and you gotta choose if you wanna be the pimp or the trick."

Junior liked Dazè's spin on life. "I'm most definitely the pimp, my nigga. All ten toes down!"

"Keep on pimping, pimpin'," Jeff chimed in.

"So, you decided what you wanna do? What you gon' do to put food on the table, Dazè?"

"I thought about what you said yesterday, how you got out with plans but that shit changed when that money got put in yo' face. Before I seen how y'all niggas moved, I wasn't sure what I wanted to do. But after watching you blow damn near twenty racks on me like it wasn't shit, I definitely wanna eat with you niggas. I wanna be a Parklawn Grinder."

Junior smiled, reaching out and shaking Dazè's hand. "Welcome to the team! Let's take a walk. I wanna introduce you to my other cousin, T-Murda, and get you some work. I think he gotta extra line too. I'mma see if I can get that for you."

Dazè and Junior left Jeff's house and were walking through Parklawn when they ran into a nigga named Jabo making a serve. He and Junior had a complicated history stemming from high school. Jabo played basketball and had lots of females. Junior fucked one of his girls, Nae-Nae. When Jabo found out, they exchanged words. Now every time they saw each other, they exchanged mean mugs.

"What's up with you and ol' boy?" Dazè asked, watching them exchange dirty looks.

"That bitch ass nigga mad that I fucked his bitch in high school. Bitch ass nigga," Junior spat. "Once we lock Parklawn down, that nigga ain't gon' be able to get money out here no more."

"I'll move that nigga around right now. Just say the word," Dazè said, ready to put in work."

"We don't got time for that nigga right now. I'm finna get you together first. Plus, I need you to call them niggas in Chicago and get this greenlight up off me."

"Say less, my nigga. I'm finna call right now." Dazè pulled out his phone and dialed a number and put it on speaker.

"Yeah?" a man answered.

"I need to holla at David."

"Who dis?"

"This Dazè."

"Oh, Dazè! What's good, nigga!? Welcome home. This D'Shon."

"D'shon, what's good, family?"

"How you doing? You coming to the city anytime soon? You know we got a blessing for you whenever you come through."

"Fa sho. That's what I wanted to talk to David about. My nigga got some funk with the mob and I wanna take care of it."

"Hold on. We ain't gon' talk on the phone. Hit me back on Facetime."

After hanging up, Dazè called him back on Facetime.

"What's this funk you talking about?"

"My nigga, Junior, said it's a green light on 'em. Something happened in Lacrosse."

D'shon nodded. "Yeah. One of the guys came up missing over there. You know the nigga that did that?"

Dazè looked at Junior. "He standing next to me right now. He said he wanna make it right."

"Hand him the phone."

Junior grabbed the phone. He and D'Shon had a brief stare off.

"How you gon' right what you did, fam? You gon' bring lil' Folks back?"

"You know that can't be done. But you wasn't there. It was me or him. I fucked with Terrance, but shit went sour. I didn't have a choice."

D'shon studied Junior's face for a moment. "You gon' have to come to the city and holla at the guys. I ain't in a position to call it off. But I can tell you that it's gon' cost you. And we probably gon' add tax."

Junior laughed. "I won't be coming to the city. That's out. But I'll pay the tax. What's the number?"

"I'mma holla at the heads and get up with Dazè. Give my nigga the phone back."

"What's good, D'Shon?"

"Keep that nigga close to you. I'mma holla at David and hit you back."

"Okay. Plenty much love."

"Love."

"That nigga talking about come to Chicago. Ain't no way I'mma go to the city where they got a hit on me at," Junior laughed. "That shit sound crazy."

"I think they just gon' hit you with the tax. And I'mma vouch for you. Niggas know I'm valid."

When they got to T-Murda's spot, Junior introduced them, got the extra phone, a Glock, and an ounce of dope for Dazè. T-Murda also had ten thousand for Junior to collect. Junior left to drop the money off. During the drive, he got a call from Dazè.

"What's good?"

"I just got off the phone with David. They want fifty racks."

"Fifty?" Junior asked, surprised by the number.

"I said the same shit. But most of the time they ain't calling no green light. I think you gotta pay it."

"Okay. I'mma grab it. How they want me to send it?"

"They want me to bring you to Chicago."

Junior laughed. "That shit ain't gon' happen, my nigga. I'm not going to Chicago. It seem like these niggas on some bullshit."

"I can't really say. But like I told you, I'm vouching for you. I just think they need to see you. Like a formality or something. They might got a few questions."

"Formality my ass. Them niggas try'na get me. I tell you what. How about I send somebody for me?"

"That might work. Who you wanna send?"

"I don't know. What you think?"

Dazè thought for a moment. "When somebody wanna meet the president, he sends a diplomat on his behalf. I think you gotta move on that level. You gotta send family."

"John?"

"Maybe. Or what about Renae? She a civilian. I can guarantee that won't nothing happen to her."

Junior thought for a moment. "She probably won't do it. But I'mma call her and see what she say."

After ending the call with Dazè, Junior called his sister.

"What?" she answered with plenty of attitude.

"I need you to do me a favor."

"Nigga, I ain't doing shit for you. Not after you was calling me bitches and hoes last night. And when I see you, I'm bussing you in yo' shit."

"Man, you ain't gon' do shit. Shut up, nigga. But I need yo' help for real. I need you to go to Chicago with Dazè and make a drop for me."

Her tone changed when he mentioned Dazè. "Make a drop with Dazè? Some dope?"

"Nah. Some money. They want fifty to take this greenlight off me."

"When do you want us to leave?"

***

"I ain't gon' get shot or kidnapped, am I?" Renae asked, glancing over toward the passenger seat.

"Nah, you good," Dazè laughed. "You with me. For somebody to get to you, they gotta go through me first. And that ain't easy."

Renae looked at the way the T-shirt was hugging his biceps. "So, you my bodyguard? Like the white man in the movie with Whitney Houston?"

"I can be Kevin Costner or whoever else you want me to be," Dazè said, meeting and holding her gaze.

Renae smiled before turning her attention back to the highway. "Is they really gon' leave my brother alone after you give them this money?"

"Yeah. We gotta honor our word. That's what separates real G's from everybody else. If we say we gon' do something, we gotta do it. You might not think it because of what you see out here, but real gangstas believe in honor."

"These niggas out here don't believe in nothing. They will finesse anybody if they get the chance. Nowadays, finessing is part of the game."

"Not with me. I keep my word. That's all a nigga got in this world is his word and his balls. And I don't break mine for nobody."

"You different. I don't think I ever met anybody like you."

Dazè smiled. "That's how it's supposed to be. I'm cut from a rare cloth."

They became silent for a moment.

"So, do you got a nigga, Renae?"

She frowned and smiled. "Ooh, why you try'na get all in my business?"

"Because I wanna make yo' business my business. That's how people get to know each other."

"My business yo' business, huh?" she laughed. "No, I don't have a man. Do you have a girl?"

"Nah. I don't really got time to be try'na find a girl. I gotta figure out life. Figure out what I want and what I like. I went to the joint when I was fifteen. Now I'm twenty-eight. It's still a lot of shit I don't know about life. Shit that I gotta figure out."

"Damn, I can't believe you did thirteen years. How the fuck you do it, man. How come you didn't go crazy?"

"How you know I ain't crazy?" Dazè cracked.

Renae gave him a 'don't make me fuck you up' look.

"I'm just bullshitting," he laughed. "It's a saying that I like. 'The journey of a thousand miles starts with a single step.' That means that we can do anything. You just gotta start and keep going."

Renae nodded. "When you put it like that, it seem like we can do anything."

"That's exactly the point, Renae. We can do anything. The only limit is in yo' head. If you think you can do anything, then you will. I think it's just that simple. What is something that you wanna do that you don't think you can do?"

Renae thought for a moment. "I want a million dollars."

Dazè laughed. "Shit, we got the same goal. And I bet you if we put our heads together, we could do it."

Renae took her eyes off the road to look at him. "Are you serious? You want to put our heads together?"

Dazè leaned over and kissed her lips. "That's my answer."

Renae blushed. "Damn, nigga. You got a way with words."

Dazè and Renae talked and vibed all the way to Chicago. When she pulled into the city, Dazè called David and got directions to the drop. It was a blue and white house on 73rd and Ada, Chicago's south side. There were a few niggas on the porch who looked serious.

"Stay right here," Dazè said, tucking the Glock 40 in his waist and grabbing the small Gucci tote with fifty G's before getting out of the car.

"What's good, fam? Who you looking for?" one of the niggas on the porch asked.

"I'm Dazè. I'm looking for David."

"He waiting on you. Go in."

Dazè stepped into the house and saw a bunch of niggas sitting around the living room. He recognized two of them from pictures he had gotten while in prison. The heavyset, dark-skinned nigga with long dreads was D'Shon. David was a tall, slim nigga with a nappy afro.

"Dazè! Gimmie some love, nigga!" D'shon smiled, welcoming him with a hug.

David came over to hug him next. "What's good, Dazè? I see you looking good, Folks. Welcome home!"

"Thank y'all for the love. And it feel good to be out. So, so good!"

"I know it do. What you do? Fifteen, right?" David asked.

"Thirteen. But shit, it felt like fifteen."

"I hear you, my nigga. Come in and sit down. Let me introduce you to some of the guys," D'Shon said, moving over to the couches. After introducing Dazè to the guys, they got down to business.

"So, where is the nigga that changed lil' Folks?" D'shon asked.

"I couldn't get him to come. He a cautious nigga. But he did send the bread," Dazè said, sitting the bag on the table.

"Who in the car?" David asked.

Dazè was hoping to keep Renae out of it. "That's Renae. Junior's sister."

David nodded toward one of his niggas. "Tell her to come in." Then he turned back to Dazè. "I wanted that nigga to come so I could see how it went down. All we know is they ran from the law and Terrance got found in some woods the next day. What he tell you?"

"He said him and Terrance was cool. Said they went on moves and put in work together. Then he said fam got disrespectful one day and said he was a bitch, or some shit like that. He let it slide, but he said when Folks tried to put hands on him, that crossed the line. After that, they was enemies. He caught fam slipping and popped 'em."

"You think he was telling the truth?" D'shon asked. "Some niggas a change the story to make they self look a certain way."

"I think he was being a hunnit. He said Terrance was a demon and he couldn't play with him."

"Yeah. Lil' Folks was a young savage," David said. "And we gon' accept yo' version of this. But, since you spoke up for Junior and we calling this off on yo' behalf, we gon' need you to do something for us."

Dazè nodded. "You know I got y'all."

"I know. I'mma text you later tonight. Stay in the city. Be ready."

Then the door opened and Renae walked in.

"Come in, shorty. Have a seat next to Dazè," D'Shon said.

Renae walked nervously over to Dazè and sat next to him.

"You Junior sister, right?" David asked.

Renae nodded. "Yeah."

"Tell yo' brother that we gon' give him a pass," Dave began. "But if he have another situation with the guys, especially niggas that's in the books, he gotta stand down and holla at us. If some shit like this happen again, we ain't giving out no more passes. You hear me?"

Renae nodded. "Yeah, I hear you. I'mma tell him."

"Good," he said, reaching for the bag of money. "Dazè, you an outstanding member. Everything you did while you was doing yo' time, we heard about and took heed to. Every nigga that ran across yo' path spoke highly of you. So I'mma give you half of what Junior gave to the mob. Thanks for yo' service, family."

156

After accepting the money, Dazè and Renae left. He called Junior to tell him the news.

"What happened, Dazè? Am I good?"

"We just left. And you good. They up off you. But it's a catch."

"A catch?" Junior asked.

Dazè looked at Renae as he spoke. "Yeah. They want me to stay in the city tonight and make a move."

"What kinda move?" Renae and Junior asked at the same time.

"They didn't say. They gon' let me know later."

"You trust 'em?" Junior asked.

"Yeah. These some govs. They the real big homies. Plus, it's part of getting that greenlight off you. I'm good. I got it."

"A'ight. Let me know if you need anything."

"You know it," Dazè said, about to end the call.

"And they said don't shoot no more of they niggas or they gon' shoot yo' stupid ass," Renae added.

"Fuck you, nigga. And when you come back home, I'm busting you in yo' shit," Junior threatened. "Aight, Dazè. Get at me later."

"I thought them niggas was gon' kill me," Renae confessed after Dazè hung up the phone. "I was scared as hell when that nigga came and got me."

He laughed. "How you gon' talk all that shit to yo' brother but be scared of other niggas?"

"Shit, that's my brother. I know he ain't gon' hurt me. But them other niggas, I wasn't sure. I seen the news. These niggas in Chicago don't play."

"I told you I wasn't gon' let nothing happen to you. I'm yo' bodyguard." Dazè smiled.

Renae glanced over and saw Dazè watching her. Being under his gaze made her insides turn to mush. "Why you looking at me like that?"

"Because I like looking at you. Because you pretty."

She blushed, smiling so wide that she thought her lips might crack. "Thank you."

"You ever been shopping in downtown Chicago?" he asked.

"Nah. This is my first time here."

"Mine too. How about we take a detour and check out the city. I just got free bands. You wanna go shopping?"

"Nigga, is that even a real question? Of course, I wanna go shopping!"

Renae and Dazè ended up spending the rest of the day exploring downtown Chicago and shopping. After blowing ten bands, Dazè rented a suite at Trump Tower for them to spend the night.

"Damn, this muthafucka is plush as a bitch!" Dazè said, amazed by the luxurious atmosphere of the hotel suite. "And it's a mutha-fuckin' jacuzzi in this bitch!"

"They even gave us a bottle of champagne. Look," Renae said, pointing to the bottle of liquor sitting on ice on the kitchen island.

"Shit, you down to pop the bottle and jump in this jacuzzi?"

Renae looked at him like he was crazy. "Nigga, why you keep asking me these crazy ass questions?! Let's go!"

Renae grabbed the bottle and two glasses before they stripped down to their underwear and climbed in the hot tub.

"This some boss ass shit right here." Dazè smiled while sipping champagne. "I never thought I would be doing shit like this on my second day out. This shit feel unreal. Like I'm dreaming."

Renae reached over and pinched him on the leg.

"Ah, shit! Why you do that?" he asked.

"To show you that you wasn't dreaming," Renae giggled.

Dazè reached under the water and pinched her back.

"Ouch! Why you pinch me?"

"To make sure it was real for you too," he laughed.

They began pinching each other and playing in the water. A few moments later, the atmosphere changed as sexual energy danced around them. When their lips met, it felt like a burst of electricity traveled through their bodies. Dazè snatched Renae onto his lap and they made out passionately, his hands roaming all over her body while she grinded on his lap. Renae moved her face to lick his neck and whisper in his ear.

"Let me ride you in this jacuzzi," she whispered.

"Let me take my boxers off."

She moved to stand up, and they both removed their underwear before she sat back on his lap. Their lips found each other's again as she sat down on him. Then she reached down and allowed him inside.

"Oh shit, Dazè!" she moaned as he slid deep.

"Damn," Dazè moaned with her, gripping her hips and loving the feel of her insides as she rode him in the jacuzzi.

It didn't take long for her to get used to him being inside her walls. For Renae, she felt like he belonged inside her. He was a perfect fit, and she couldn't get enough. The water splashed all around them as they continued to kiss and Renae worked her hips. Dazè's hands slid lower, gripping her ass and pulling her into him as he pushed into her. Their motions got faster with every thrust, push, and pull. A few moments later, they both reach their sexual peaks.

"Oh, Dazè! Oh, Dazè!" Renae moaned loudly as the orgasm rushed through her body.

The orgasm made her walls clench and she gripped Dazè's dick tightly, making him bust with her. After his balls were drained, Dazè wondered if it was possible to fall in love with someone in two days.

***

Dazè was awakened by his phone vibrating. The clock on the screen read 2:13 a.m. There was a text from D'Shon asking for his location. Dazè texted back that he was at the Trump Tower. Another text came telling him to be ready in thirty minutes. After checking to make sure Renae was still asleep, Dazè slid out of bed and hit the bathroom. He took a piss and splashed some cold water on his face to wake up. When he walked back into the room, Renae was sitting up.

"That was the call?" she asked.

"Yeah. They gon' pick me up in thirty minutes," he said while sliding into his pants.

"You don't think it's strange that they calling you at two o'clock in the morning?"

"I don't think it's strange. I think it's deadly."

"And you cool with that? You just got out of prison yesterday and you already getting in some bullshit."

Dazè sat on the bed next to her. "I'm not one of them work a job ass niggas, Renae. I just did thirteen years in a maximum-security prison. A kind gesture from a nigga you fuck with is getting a shank. I breathed violence almost every single fucking day. When a nigga disrespect you, you don't fold. You make that nigga bleed. That was my life since I was fifteen years old. This gangsta shit is what I do. I can't turn it off, baby. And if you fuck with me, this is what I am."

Renae didn't know what to say. How could she tell a gangsta not to be a gangsta? That was like telling someone not to breathe. Or telling a bird not to fly.

"I'mma be okay, Renae. Everything that I been through prepared me for this life. Plus, this part of the deal to keep your brother alive. You do want me to help your brother, right?"

"You know I do. I just want you to be safe."

Dazè picked up the Glock that he got from Junior. "That's what this is for."

When he got the text from D'Shon, Dazè left the suite and found a black BMW parked at the curb. D'Shon was waiting inside. "What's good, G? You ready to move?"

"I stay ready so I won't have to get ready," Dazè said as he slid into the passenger seat.

"I can love that." D'Shon smiled, handing Dazè a black 357 revolver as he pulled away from the curb. "I need you to put in some work on this nigga, Bee-Bee. Bitch ass fag set up one of the guys to get hit and he don't think we know about it. We been knew but been waiting on the right time. I need you to go in there and smoke him and whoever else in the house."

Dazè checked to make sure the revolver was loaded. "How many people in the house?"

"Should be just him and maybe a lil' freak. This one of the nation houses and it's his turn to hustle. He think you dropping him off some work. Tell him yo' name Free."

Dazè nodded. "I got it."

D'shon glanced over at him, assessing his demeanor. "You sure you up for this, Dazè? You just got out and I understand if you a lil' nervous or scared."

Dazè chuckled. "Let me tell you the truth about nervousness and fear, family. They natural reactions to stressful situations. If a nigga about to do something dangerous and he not nervous or a little fearful, that nigga is lying. The key to it is harnessing those feelings and using them to your advantage. Fear releases adrenaline. Adrenaline makes you stronger and faster. And that makes me more dangerous."

D'shon gave an approving nod. "I heard you was up top mentally, but I see that was an understatement. You a real-life nigga's worst nightmare. I'mma let the guys know about yo' performance."

D'Shon showed Dazè where Bee-Bee was staying before driving two blocks over and parking. Dazè moved with a purpose when he left the BMW, walking quickly to the spot. He walked upon the porch and knocked. Someone answered a few moments later. "Who dat?"

"It's Free. I got that for you," Dazè said, using the name D'Shon told him. Locks clicked and the door opened a moment later. A buff dark-skinned nigga with a nappy afro stood in the doorway.

"What's good, fam? Come in."

Dazè stepped into the house, taking in his surroundings while looking for signs of someone else being there. He didn't see anybody. "Damn, my nigga. You up in here solo? Where the lil' thottys at?"

"Nah, I ain't on shit. Just my lil' dip in the room."

"One-woman man, huh?" Dazè laughed. "Where the bathroom at? Let me piss real quick."

Bee-Bee gave a suspicious look before pointing toward the back of the house. "The bathroom down the hallway."

Dazè took a couple of steps toward the hallway before spinning around with the 357 in his grip. Bee-Bee froze, terror lighting his eyes.

Pop!

A single shot to the forehead dropped the big man where he stood. Dazè raced toward the bedroom and kicked the door open. A half-naked female had just picked up a silver automatic from the bedside table. She and Dazè pointed guns at each other at the same time, both squeezing triggers.

Pop!

Clap!

The bullet from her automatic flew by Dazè's head, missing him by inches, but the 357 slug hit her in the chest. While she was falling onto the bed, Dazè shot her three more times before leaving the house in a hurry. He speed walked two blocks over to where D'Shon waited in the BMW.

"It's done," he said calmly as he hopped in the passenger seat.

D'Shon had to make sure. "He dead, right?"

Dazè looked him in his eyes. "Yeah. Him and the bitch. Let's go."

D'shon took his word and drove away. "We gon' drive over the bridge so you can get rid of that burner in the river."

Chapter 10

Dazè couldn't sleep. He kept thinking about killing Bee-Bee and his girl. He had killed before while in prison. Twice. Killing with a shank was different than killing with a gun. Killing with a shank was up close and personal. You had to make sure you stabbed in the right spot. Killing by gun was much easier. Just point and squeeze. Let the bullets do the work. Tonight was the first time he had ever killed someone with a gun. He played the scenes in his head over and over, slowing them down and remembering how the bullets pierced their flesh. Killing someone in real life looked different than in the movies. There was no blood spraying or heads exploding. Just a slapping sound as bullets tore into flesh. And as he thought about the murders, he realized that he preferred killing with a shank. And that made him wonder if he was crazy. Who sat up all night thinking about the people they killed? Or realized that they preferred stabbing someone over shooting them? A crazy person.

His phone ringing pulled him from the murderous thoughts. He glanced at the clock first. It was 9:46. Junior's name showed on the screen. He looked at Renae sleeping and thought about not answering. He wasn't sure how Junior would react to him fucking his sister. But trying to hide it wouldn't be gangsta. So, he answered.

"What's good, fam?"

"I'm on my way to the hood to make this move. Where you at, nigga?"

Dazè glanced at Renae again. "We still in Chicago." He winced.

There was a slight pause on Junior's end. "Renae with you?"

Dazè chuckled. "Yeah. She right here. Sleep."

"On what, you fucked my sister, nigga?" Junior laughed.

"My bad, fam. It just happened. We just hit it off, you know what I'm saying? She my type."

"I bet," Junior laughed again. "I can't believe you fucked my sister, nigga. But I can't trip. Me and Tamar used to have a little thing back in the day."

"On what?" Dazè asked, surprised.

"It wasn't really shit. I never fucked. Some teenage shit. But listen, I gotta get to this money. What happened with that move? You good?"

"Yeah, I took care of that. Everything is everything."

"My nigga!" Junior cheered. "Get up with me when y'all get back in the city."

"I will. Love."

"What he say?" Renae asked after Dazè hung up the phone.

"I thought you was just sleep."

"I woke up when yo' phone rang. I just kept my eyes closed. What he say?"

"Nothing really. That he wasn't tripping and he used to fuck with Tamar back in the day."

Renae's eyes grew wide. "I forgot that him and Tamar did have a little thing back in the day. I don't think it was nothing serious though."

"That's what he said."

"That's good that he ain't gon' be on no bullshit, 'cause I sho don't want that nigga all up in my business."

"That's what brothers supposed to do. If I was out when Serena and Tamar started fucking, I would have been all in they business. Woulda beat up all they lil' boyfriends, too," he laughed.

"You crazy, nigga," Renae giggled. "What did you go to jail for anyway? Did you kill somebody?"

Dazè shook his head. "Nah, I didn't. Somebody died, but I didn't do it. A couple of my niggas stomped a dope fiend to death. I was there, but I didn't touch him. Then somebody told on one of my niggas, who I thought was my nigga. Then him and his mama told the police I did it. Testified on me in court and everything. If I find that nigga, I'mma blow his shit out."

Renae was blown away by the story. "Damn! You did all that time for some shit that you didn't do?"

"Shit, I didn't have no choice. I wasn't gon' snitch. I had to take the hit. I ain't built like these niggas out here. I wasn't finna get out on a tell. I told you, I'm rare."

"You right about that, because I woulda told on they ass," Renae laughed. "I ain't doing no time for something I didn't do."

Dazè gave her a serious look. "Let me tell you something, Renae. If you gon' be fucking with me, don't ever say no bullshit like that again."

Renae was surprised by how serious he had become. "I was just playing, Dazè. Damn."

"I don't play about that telling shit. Not even a little bit. I got told on. That shit ain't nothing to joke about."

"Okay. My bad. Who was the nigga that told on you?"

"Bitch ass nigga name Jason. He used to live on 44th and Hope back in the day. Black and fat, ugly nigga. I'mma find his ass one day."

Renae thought for a moment. "I think I remember Jason. Ain't his mama name Carolyn or something like that?"

"Yeah, that's her. She fat, black, and ugly too. You know how to find him or her?"

"I don't know. Shit, it really ain't that hard to find nobody now. Everybody on Facebook."

Darkness entered Dazè's eyes. "Can I trust you?"

Renae sat up and looked in his eyes, sensing the seriousness of the moment. "I ride for niggas that I got love for. Ask Junior. When some niggas shot at him, I was standing on the front line with a chopper."

Even though the moment was serious, Dazè laughed. "On what, you was on the front line with a chopper?"

"On everything I love. I told you I don't play about people that I love."

Dazè just stared into her eyes, thinking the same thought from last night. Was it really possible to fall in love in two days?

***

Junior was standing in front of his mother's house with John, Dazè, and T-Murda when Larena's white Benz pulled up and parked. Larena hopped out with her sister, Shaneen. Both of them looked good enough to eat.

"Larena! Hey, baby. How you doing?" Junior asked, greeting the dime piece with a hug.

"I'm good. Could be a lot better though," she said before giving him a peck on the lips.

"Tell me what could make it better. You deserve the world."

"I don't need the whole world to make me better. You in my bed later is fine with me." She smiled.

"I'mma make that happen," he said before turning to her sister. "Shaneen, what's good? Been a minute."

"I'm good. Working and taking care of my kids. When Larena told me she was coming over, I had to jump in with her. Where is Lo-Dog?"

"I don't know. I ain't seen that nigga in a couple days. Ask T-Murda," Junior said before turning to Larena. "What's good with you? How was work?"

"It was okay. Dealing with these bad ass teenagers can be hard some days. But today was a good day. What about you? What you do today?"

"Nothing exciting. Just grinding, baby."

"Well, making money is always good. Come over to the car with me. I want to talk to you about something."

They walked over to her car and leaned against it.

"What's up, baby? What's on yo' mind?" Junior asked.

"Well, I was at work talking to a coworker and she was telling me about her and her man moving in together, and it made me think about you. You still living with your mother, and I wanted to ask you if you wanted to move in with me."

Junior was throwed by the question. "Say what now?"

"Damn. I didn't think you would react like that," she said, feeling a little rejected.

"Shit, I wasn't expecting you to ask me to move in with you. That's some serious shit, and I didn't think we was that serious."

"So, tell me what we're doing, Junior. You just want to keep fucking? That's it?"

166

Junior shrugged. "Yeah. I mean, don't get me wrong, I fuck with you. You know we go way back. But I ain't ready for commitment or moving in. I thought we was just kicking it."

She crossed her arms over her chest, getting a little irritated "Well, what if I don't want to just kick it no more? What if I'm tired of just kicking it and want something more?"

Junior leaned against the car, letting out a long breath while running a hand across his face. "Damn, Larena. This ain't a good time to do this. I need some time to think. You catching feelings and changing up. I wasn't ready to have this conversation."

"You'll never be ready if we wait until the right time. There is never a right time."

"I know. But right now is really not the right time. I'm not in the headspace to have this talk right now. Let's catch up later. I'm getting money right now."

Larena got an attitude. "So that's it. Leave you alone while you hustling?"

"C'mon, Larena. Whatever this is right here, this not for us. I don't wanna go there with you."

Her green eyes flashed a shade of angry green. "You know what, Junior? I'mma leave before I say something to you that I can't take back."

And with that, she walked around to the driver's side and hopped in the car. She blew the born a couple of times, waving for her sister. Junior stood at the curb wondering what the hell just happened.

"What happened?" Shaneen asked.

"I'm still try'na figure that out," Junior said, looking confused.

"My sister falls in love fast, man. And y'all go way back. Whatever she's mad about, it stems from her being in love with you."

Junior was about to respond but stopped when he saw Quitta's Jeep turn on the block. "Damn, there go my baby mama."

"Ooh. Should we leave?" Shaneen asked, getting a little worried.

"Too late for that," Junior said, locking eyes with Quitta as she parked.

She looked pissed off as she hopped out the truck. She walked over, mugging Junior and Shaneen. "When I come back out here, this bitch better be gone," she threatened.

Junior mugged her. "Man, you better get the fuck out my face with that bullshit. This my mama house, not yours."

"You heard what I said," Quitta called as she walked in the house.

"Damn, Junior. She is mad. I think we should leave."

Junior was in his feelings about Quitta threatening him and became defiant. "Fuck her. We not together no more. She ain't finna come to my crib try'na tell me who can be over here. I don't even know why she over here without Mooka. You good."

"Okay." Shaneen shrugged. "But my sister does love you, Junior. For real. Don't shut her down. Just take how she feels into consideration when you talk to her. And don't give up on her because her feelings for you is making her crazy."

Junior laughed at her words before looking in the car and locking eyes with Larena. She looked like she wanted to cry. He was about to get in the car and talk to her when his mother, Renae, and Quitta came out of the house. They walked down the walkway headed right for him.

"Didn't I tell you this bitch better be gone when I came back outside?" Quitta asked, walking up on Junior.

He lifted a foot to stop her from walk up on him. And that's when Gail grabbed him, tackling him on the ground.

"Mama, what you doing?" Junior asked, trying to push her off him.

While he was wrestling with his mother, Quitta started punching Shaneen. Instead of fighting back, Shaneen covered up and started screaming.

"Damn! Quitta beating her ass!" T-Murda yelled excitedly, pulling out his phone to record.

"Why are you hitting me! I'm not messing with Junior!"

Quitta stopped hitting her, backing away and throwing up her hands. "Well, who is it then? Where the bitch at?"

"It's me, bitch!" Larena yelled, jumping out of the car and rushing Quitta.

Junior had just gotten from under his mother when Larena and Quitta started fighting. After the first couple of punches, it looked like it would be an even match. But that quickly changed. Quitta took Larena's punches like a champ. Larena, on the other hand, couldn't handle Quitta's heavy-handed punches. After several punches to the face, she grabbed Quitta to stop her from throwing punches.

"This what you like, Junior?! Huh? Light-skinned bitches with good hair and pretty eyes?" Quitta yelled as she began ripping at Larena's hair and digging her nails into her face.

Larena tried to run, but Quitta gave chase, punching her in the back of the head. The fight was obviously over, but Quitta wanted to humiliate Larena. Junior stepped in to break it up.

"Okay, Quitta. It's over! Chill," Junior said, grabbing her around the waist and pulling her away.

When Larena jumped in the car and drove off, Quitta turned her anger on Junior.

"Why the fuck you got these bitches out here, nigga!? Didn't I tell you that bitch better be gon'?"

"Man, I'm doing me, nigga. Fuck is you talking about? We ain't together."

"Okay. Bring another bitch over here. Let me see you with another bitch and watch what happens!" Quitta threatened.

During their exchange, a black SUV turned onto the block, driving slowly, all the windows down. Four niggas were in the truck armed to the teeth with automatic weapons. When Junior noticed the truck, it was already in front of his mother's house. He locked eyes with the driver and immediately knew he was in danger. He pushed Quitta onto the ground and ducked down as shots rang out.

Brrrreeeaaaaattt! Brrrreeeaaaaattt! Brrrreeeaaaaattt!

Tat-tat-tat-tat! Tat-tat-tat-tat-tat! Tat-tat-tat-tat-tat-tat!

Everybody outside ducked for cover. Except Dazè. He pulled the 40 from his waist and ran toward the SUV letting his trigger go. *Pop, pop, pop, pop, pop, pop, pop, pop, pop, pop!*

The truck sped away and dipped around a corner.

Junior turned to Quitta as visions of the shooting at Ron's house flashed in his head. "You good? The baby good?"

She nodded, shook up from the drive-by. "We good. Who the fuck was that?"

"Them bitch ass BGM niggas," Junior said while looking around at everyone getting up from the ground. "Y'all good?"

"We good," T-Murda said, dusting himself off as he stood.

"Oh my god! What the fuck just happened?" Gail yelled hysterically.

John wrapped his arms around his mother. "We good, Mama. We good."

"Everybody go in the house. John, you stay here and make sure they good," Junior ordered. "Dazè, slide with me."

"Wait! Where y'all going?" Renae asked.

"I'm finna find the niggas that did this and burn all them niggas," Junior promised. "Let's go, Dazè."

"Who was that?" Dazè asked as they hopped in the Lexus truck.

"That was them bitch ass BGM niggas! Them bitch ass niggas just shot up my mama house! I'm killing all them niggas," Junior said as he pulled out his phone and called Fifty.

"My nigga! What's good?" he answered.

"These bitch ass BGM niggas just shot up my mama house, Fif. Where you at?"

"They shot up Gail house!? On what?" Fifty asked, not believing what he just heard.

"On everything I love. My mama was outside. She could'da got hit. I'm finna slide on these niggas. Where you at?"

"I'm on my way to the crib right now. Meet me there."

As soon as Junior hung up the phone, it rang. It was Lo-Dog. "What up?"

"I just seen Renae live. On what, a nigga just shot up Aunty house?!"

"Man, Lo. They really did. Bitch ass BGM niggas. I'm on my way to Fifty house right now."

"Cuz, don't slide without me. I'm on my way."

Junior pulled up to Fifty's house at the same time as Fifty was pulling into the driveway. He hopped out the Lexus with murder in his eyes.

"I'm killing everybody that them niggas know. Mamas, grand-mamas, and kids. Everybody gotta go!"

"What happened, fam? How they come through?" Fifty asked as he unlocked the door.

"Bitch ass niggas did a drive-by. Everybody was outside because Quitta had just whooped my bitch. Then, soon as the fight over, these niggas slide."

"I can't believe they didn't hit nobody because we was all out in the open," Dazè said.

"Don't even trip, fam. We finna slide on them niggas ASAP. Y'all come in. Let's smoke something and plot. Did you get in contact with Lo-Dog?" Fifty asked.

"He seen Renae on live and hit me. He should be on his way. I'm killing that nigga whole family, brah. On everything I love," Junior promised as his phone rang again. It was Six. "They just shot up Mama house, brah," he answered.

"Who shot up Mama house? I seen Renae shit and thought I was tripping. Who did it?"

"BGM niggas seen us in the club on Sammy D birthday and found out where we was from and slid on us."

"What the fuck, Junior!? How the fuck you let that shit get to Mama house, nigga?" Six yelled angrily.

"Man, I ain't try'na hear that blame game shit right now, brah. Mu'fuckas almost got knocked off. I'm finna slide."

"Nah, don't do nothing. You already did enough. You shoulda been deaded that shit. It's obvious that you can't handle this shit, so I'm finna send my niggas to clean it up. Where these niggas from?"

Junior pulled the phone away from his ear, looking at it like the phone had done something wrong. "Brah, I just told you I got it. We finna slide. I'mma hit you back later," he said, ending the call before Six could say another word.

"You just hung up on Six?" Fifty laughed.

"That nigga blowing me with that shit he was talking about. I'll holla at him later. How we finna move on these niggas?"

Excitement flashed in Fifty's eyes. "Let me show y'all something," he said before disappearing toward the back of the house. He came back a few moments later with a shotgun. Junior didn't see the big deal.

"Look at this bitch!" Fifty grinned.

"It's a gauge, fam. What's so special about that?" Junior asked.

"Because this ain't no regular gauge, nigga. First of all, it's a ten gauge. And it's a riot pump. This is a semiautomatic gauge, nigga. Got air holes and a beam. And," he paused, pulling a clip from his waist. "It got a twenty-shot clip and hold five in the neck."

Dazè looked like he had fallen in love. "Damn, that's a bad muthafucka! Let me see it."

When Fifty gave him the gun, Dazè examined it like it was a precious jewel or a bad bitch. "You gotta let me use this muthafucka, Fifty. Please, my nigga!"

"That's you. I'm still in love with my Mac."

"So, how you wanna slide?" Junior asked. "I say we hit they block and drop niggas. And keep sliding and keep dropping them niggas. Let them niggas know they fucking with the wrong niggas."

Fifty shrugged. "I was gon' say kidnap one of them niggas and make him tell us who is who. But we can just keep sliding on them niggas too."

"Let's snatch one of them niggas," Dazè spoke up. "We need as much info as we can get so we can hit 'em hard and fuck up they world. Have the niggas paying us to get off they ass."

Junior nodded. "I love it."

"Where the fuck is that nigga, Lo-Dog? Call him and see where he at. I'm ready to move," Fifty said impatiently.

Junior made the call.

"Hello?" a man who wasn't Lo-Dog answered.

"Where Lo-Dog at?"

"Who is this?"

Junior frowned. "Who is this? Where Lo-Dog at?"

"This is Officer Williams with the Milwaukee Police Department. Who are you?"

Junior hung up the phone. "I think the police got Lo-Dog!"

Fifty looked shocked. "How you know?"

"'Cause they just answered his phone."

All of their eyes bucked as they looked at one another.

"Cut that phone off and get rid of it!" Fifty yelled.

Junior hurried up and hit the power.

"If they got his phone, he probably ain't finna show up here," Dazè said.

"Let's go get these niggas!"

After changing into dark clothes and putting on face masks, they left Fifty's house and hopped in his Jeep. The first thing they had to do was steal a car. Fifty dropped Junior off at the nearest gas station and parked across the street. Junior didn't waste time. He spotted a woman standing near a white Chevy truck and approached. The woman must've sensed his intentions because as soon as they locked eyes, she began to panic.

"Wait! No, don't take my car!"

Junior pulled his pistol and pushed her away from the truck. "Move, bitch!"

The keys were already in the ignition. He started the SUV and burned rubber out of the gas station, the gas nozzle slapping ground when it was yanked from the truck. Fifty followed him for a couple of blocks before he pulled over and let them in. Their next stop was 40th and Center. BGM headquarters. They drove slowly down the block looking for anybody wearing a BGM chain or gear.

"There go one of them niggas!" Dazè pointed from the back seat.

A short and stocky dark-skinned nigga with shoulder-length dreads was jogging down a porch, headed to a black Cadillac. He wore a custom T-shirt with BGM on the front. Junior drove toward the Cadillac and almost ran the nigga over before bringing the truck to a stop.

"What the fuck you doing, nigga?!" the BGM nigga yelled.

Fifty jumped out and put the Mac in his face. "Shut yo' bitch ass up and get in!"

Terror filled the nigga's wide eyes as he thought about running.

Fifty grabbed him by the collar and shoved him toward the back door. "I dare you to try to run, nigga!"

Before the nigga could make up his mind, Dazè opened the back door and snatched him into the truck.

"Aye! Hold on! What's going on, fam?" he panicked.

When Fifty hopped back in the passenger seat, Junior sped away. Fifty leaned over the passenger seat, pointing the Mac in the BGM nigga's face. "Who came and shot up Parklawn earlier, nigga?"

"I don't know nothing about that. I just came outside," he said, looking at the gun like it was a deadly snake.

Dazè backhanded the nigga. "Quit lying, nigga! Who the fuck came and shot up my hood? Where them niggas at?"

"C'mon, fam. I'm telling y'all I don't know nothing. On my mama."

Fifty slapped him with the Mac a couple of times, making him cover up. "You better tell us something, nigga! Who was it?"

"C'mon, fam! Please! I don't know!"

Dazè turned toward the nigga, grabbing the driver's seat and his seat to gain leverage, and started stomping the nigga. He kicked him in the face and upside the head. When he covered up his face and head, Dazè started kicking his body. In the ribs, stomach, and arms, until the nigga was crouched in a ball between the passenger and back seat.

"Okay! Okay! I'mma tell you! Okay!" he cried.

"Talk, nigga," Dazè said.

"If I tell y'all, y'all gon' let me go?"

Dazè looked at Fifty and smiled. "Yeah. We gon' let you go."

He removed his hands slowly from covering his head to peek up at Dazè. "On what, you gon' let me go?"

"That's my word. We ain't got no beef with you. We want the shooters."

The nigga stayed in a ball on the floor and spilled the beans. "It was Kevo n'em. They said y'all killed Fredo."

"Who the fuck is Kevo?" Junior asked.

"He seen y'all in the club the other night. He was the one that found out y'all was from Parklawn."

"Where he live?" Fifty asked.

"He stay with his baby mama on 41st. A green and white house."

"Who was the niggas that was with him?" Dazè asked.

"D-Ray, Tweezy, and Deonte. They all shooters."

"Where they live?"

"They all live on 40th. D-Ray stay with his pops in the second house from the corner. Tweezy live in the white house a couple houses away. And Deonte live across the street. The house with the white Audi parked on the side."

Dazè looked at Fifty and Junior to see if they had any more questions. "Y'all good?"

Fifty nodded. "Yeah. We good."

"I'm finna turn in this alley and drop you off. You bet not say nothing to yo' niggas or we coming back and burning yo' bitch ass."

"I ain't gon' say nothing. I don't wanna die."

Junior pulled into the next alley and stopped. "Get out, nigga."

The nigga moved quickly, hopping out of the SUV and taking off running. Dazè grabbed the riot pump from the rear seat and aimed it at his back.

"RICKY!" Fifty yelled, mocking the ghetto classic *Boyz N The Hood*.

Kaboom!

A long stream of fire shot from the barrel as the riot pump blasted. The slug tore into the nigga's back, knocking him to the ground.

"I love this muthafucka." Dazè grinned, kissing the weapon as Junior sped away.

After taking care of the snitch, the Parklawn killers went back to Fifty's house to discuss how they would kill the other BGM niggas.

"I say we hit Kevo first. He seem like the one that's calling the shots. The other niggas just shooters," Fifty said.

Junior and Dazè nodded.

"Sound good to me," Junior said. "Hit him tonight and get them other niggas later."

"I like it," Dazè said while pulling out his phone. "This yo' sister, fam," he told Junior before answering. "What up?"

"Dazè, this Quitta. Where Junior at?"

"This yo' BM," Dazè said, handing him the phone.

"Hello?"

"Why you not answering yo' phone? I been try'na call you?"

"I turned it off. The police answered Lo-Dog's phone when I tried to call him. I ain't fucking with that phone no more. I gotta get a new line. What's up, though? You good?"

"Nah, I ain't good. I'm scared as hell. I'm taking Mooka and going to Lacrosse tonight. Them niggas know who we is and I'm leaving. Is you coming with us?"

"Nah. I can't go. I gotta slide on these niggas. Y'all go. I'mma call you as soon as I get another line."

"Whatever, nigga. I need some money to get us straight."

"I told you I'm on something right now. I'mma send it by Cashapp or PayPal."

"I hate yo' stankin' ass," she said before hanging up.

Junior let out an angry breath.

"You good?" Dazè asked.

Junior refused to give Quitta any of his energy. "Yeah. Let's go get this bitch ass nigga Kevo."

They waited until the sun went down to pay Kevo a visit. Junior, Dazè, and Fifty crept on the side of the house, looking through windows to see how many people were in the house before meeting in the backyard to discuss the plan.

"It's Kevo, another nigga, the bitch, and they shorties," Junior confirmed.

"Blow the locks off with the gauge and we running in, killing shit," Fifty said, a blood lust in his eyes.

Dazè nodded, gripping the shotgun.

176

"And we killing everybody. Kids and all," Junior said, making sure everybody was on the same page.

"Everybody gotta go," Dazè affirmed.

The killers walked to the back door. Dazè aimed the gauge at the locks and fired.

Kaboom! Kaboom!

The locks exploded and wood splintered. Junior kicked the door open and ran into the house letting his gun talk.

J-Blunt

Chapter 11

"Mama, wake up. I'm hungry."

Quitta opened her eyes to Mooka shoving her awake. "Okay. Hold on. Give me one minute."

After yawning and stretching, Quitta grabbed her phone to check the time, 7:24 a.m.

"Can I have some cereal?" Mooka asked, rushing her up from the couch without actually telling her to get her ass up.

"Let's go see what they got," Quitta said as she got up from the couch and took Mooka to the kitchen. She searched the cabinets and found a box of Captain Crunch. After making Mooka a bowl of cereal, she sat at the table with him and checked her phone. There was a text from Junior. He sent her some money and would send more later.

"When is my daddy coming?" Mooka asked.

"I don't know. Hopefully soon."

"Can you call him so I can talk to him?"

"I'mma call him later. He probably still sleep."

"How long we gotta stay with Uncle Ron?"

"Mooka, you asking me too many questions. Just eat your cereal. I'm try'na think," Quitta snapped, stressed by her situation.

Mooka could hear the frustration in his mother's voice and decided that it was best to focus on eating the red and blue dots in his cereal. Quitta searched through social media and the news to see if she could piece together what Junior and his niggas did last night as retaliation for the shooting at his mother's house. Milwaukee had three shootings last night. A man was shot and killed at a bar. Another man was killed on the south side. And there was a mass killing in which five people died, three adults and two kids. Quitta lifted a hand to her mouth, horrified by the story. She knew that was Junior.

"Damn, you woke early," Ron said as he walked in the kitchen.

"Mooka was hungry. Nigga woke me up," Quitta griped.

"G'morning, Uncle Ron!" Mooka yelled.

"Sup, lil' nigga! Who told you you can eat my Captain Crunch?"

Mooka pointed his spoon at Quitta. "My mama."

"Snitch," Quitta laughed.

Ron grabbed the box of cereal and poured some in his hand. "You figure out what you wanna do?" he asked while smacking on the dry cereal.

"I guess I'mma find a house and lay my ass down until I have this baby. Ain't really too much else I can do. I just needed to get the fuck out of Milwaukee. Them BGM niggas ain't finna get me."

"Yeah, that sound like the best move. Did Junior send you the money?"

"I didn't check yet. Let me see." She checked her bank account and found a five-thousand-dollar transfer. "He sent me five thousand."

"That's it?" Ron asked. "Ain't he the brick man now?"

"For now, yeah. He gon' send more later. Do you know who mentioned his name to the police for that situation with Terrance? The police in Milwaukee asking about it."

Ron looked surprised. "Nah, I ain't heard nothing about it. What they say?"

"I'm finna tell you something and you bet not say nothing to nobody," Quitta warned.

Ron knew he was about to hear some good shit. "On my kids, I ain't gon' say nothing. What happened?"

Quitta looked at Mooka and decided he didn't need to hear what she was about to say. "Let's go in the living room."

When they were away from Mooka, she confided in her brother.

"Me and Junior had a fight after I went through his phone and called the bitch he was cheating on me with. When he left, I called the police on his ass and told them he had a gun."

Ron's eyes grew wide. "On what? Why would you try to send yo' baby daddy to the joint?"

"I was mad. I caught him cheating on me and we had a fight. I wanted to hurt his ass any way I could. But they didn't catch him with the gun. They let him go that night. But the detective said somebody up here said something about him killing Terrance. He said this detective is on his ass about it."

"Damn, that's fucked up," Ron gasped. "I ain't heard nothing about it, but I'mma ask around. This a little ass town, so somebody know something."

"Let me know if you hear something, because I ain't try'na be taking my kids to see they daddy in jail."

"I got you. Right now I'm finna go take a shit and shower," Ron said before walking away.

"I didn't need to know that, Ron," Quitta called after him.

***

Later that day, Quitta went shopping to buy some things for her and Mooka. When the night came, Rakisha talked Quitta into going to a friend's birthday party. With nothing else to do, she agreed. The party turned out to be a small get together with about ten people. Since she was pregnant and couldn't drink, Quitta couldn't really enjoy herself and ended up spending most of the party searching through her phone. Then the doorbell rang and got her attention.

"Hey, Quitta, can you get that for me?" Megan, the birthday girl and homeowner, asked.

Quitta reluctantly got up from the couch and walked to the door. "Who is it?"

"Steph."

Quitta thought she was hearing shit and looked out the peephole. Sure enough, it was her ex-boyfriend. She began to panic as she remembered calling the police on him and going to get Junior.

"Who is it?" Megan asked.

"Uh, I don't know. I gotta use the bathroom," Quitta said before running to the bathroom and locking the door. "Oh, shit! Oh, shit!" she panicked, damn near hyperventilating while pacing the bathroom. A moment later, there was a knock on the door.

"Quitta, you good?" Rakisha asked.

"Uh, no. I mean, yeah. Shit, I don't know," Quitta groaned, feeling like she was about to throw up.

"Unlock the door and let me in."

"Where is Steph?"

181

"He in the living room. Girl, let me in."

Quitta unlocked the door and opened it slowly, peering out to make sure Rakisha was alone. When she didn't see Steph, she grabbed Rakisha into the bathroom and locked the door. "What the fuck is he doing out there? Do he know I'm in here?"

Rakisha burst out laughing. "Girl, calm down. I told him you was in Lacrosse."

Quitta got mad at Rakisha. "Bitch, why the fuck would you do that?"

"Because he wanted to talk to you. He been asking about you ever since you left. I always told him I didn't know where you was because you was with Junior. But now that y'all broke up and he in Milwaukee and you up here, shit, I figured it wasn't nothing wrong with you talking to him."

"Well, bitch, you thought wrong. I took his money and gave it to Junior and sent him to jail. Damn, why the fuck you do this shit?"

"Girl, Steph ain't gon' do nothing to—"

They were interrupted by a knock on the door.

Quitta grabbed Rakisha in a hug. "Oh my god! I'm scared!" she whispered.

"Let me go, bitch," Rakisha laughed, pushing Quitta away. "Who is it?"

"It's Steph."

After pushing Quitta away, Rakisha opened the door. "What's up, nigga?"

Steph spoke to Rakisha, but his eyes were on Quitta. "I'm good. How you feeling?"

"I'm good. I guess y'all need to talk. I'mma leave."

Quitta reached for Rakisha, trying to keep her in the bathroom. "Wait!"

Steph laughed and lifted his hands, palms up. "I just wanna talk, Quitta. Let her go."

Quitta reluctantly let Rakisha go and moved to the back of the bathroom. When Rakisha left, Steph walked in and sat on the sink, closing the door. He was a short and slim nigga with light brown skin, and his short dreadlocks had gold tips. He wore designer clothes and an icy watch.

"Sup, Quitta? How you been?"

"I'm okay," Quitta said nervously, looking around at everything in the bathroom except Steph.

"You look good. Junior must be taking good care of you."

Quitta shrugged. "I guess. We not together no more,' so... I'm just taking care of myself."

Silence enveloped them for a few moments, Steph just staring at her. Quitta could feel his eyes upon her and slowly met his stare.

"I'm sorry for getting you locked up," she said.

Steph laughed. "No you ain't. You wanted yo' man back. I shoulda recognized that and let you go, but I guess I'mma sucka for love. Probably won't be the last time I follow my heart instead of my head."

"So, you not mad?" Quitta asked, relaxing a little and sitting on the toilet.

"Not anymore. At first I was pissed off and wanted to fuck you and Junior up. But as time went by, the pain went away, and I realized that being mad at you wasn't gon' change what happened. So, I let it go."

A knock on the interrupted them.

"Who is it?" Quitta asked.

"It's Amy. Can I talk to Steph for a moment?"

"She want some food, but she ain't got no money," Steph told Quitta.

"Wait, Amy. He'll be out in a minute," Quitta yelled. "She can wait a couple of minutes. We talking right now."

"It don't matter to me." Steph shrugged.

"So, where you been? We was looking for you."

"I heard Junior was running with Terrance crazy ass. Once I robbed y'all house, I went back home. I knew them niggas was gon' kill me. I ain't with that shooter shit. I pay niggas to put in work for me, but wasn't nobody gon' merk Terrance, so I left. Then I heard yo' nigga killed Terrance."

"Who told you that?"

"I don't remember. Is it true?"

Quitta didn't answer.

"Damn, he did do it, huh?" Steph surmised, taking the silence as a yes. "So, what you doing up here? Why you come back?"

Quitta looked away. "Me and Junior got into some shit. Got the police looking for me and niggas try'na kill me. I had to get the fuck up outta Milwaukee. I gotta raise my kids."

Steph looked surprised. "Kids?"

"Yeah. I'm two months pregnant."

Steph laughed. "I asked you to have my baby, remember? You said you didn't want to have no more kids."

Quitta didn't know how to respond, so silence filled the bathroom again. Until there was another knock on the door.

"Steph, can I talk to you real quick?" Amy asked.

Steph opened the door. "What up, Amy?"

"Can you just give it to me? Just a piece. I'll pay you tomorrow. I swear to God."

Steph shook his head. "That ain't how this work, baby. Plus, you still owe me."

"C'mon, Steph. I know I still owe you, but—"

"Damn, girl!" Quitta yelled, going in her pocket and pulling out some money. "How much two pieces cost?"

"I only got fifties," Steph said.

Quitta gave him fifty dollars. "Sell me one."

Steph gave Quitta a pack and Quitta gave it to Amy.

"Bye!"

"Thanks, Quitta!" The addict smiled before leaving.

"That was real generous," Steph said, handing Quitta the fifty. "I don't want your money. I just wanted to ask you one question."

"Ask me," Quitta said, tucking the fifty.

Steph looked into her eyes for a few moments. "Was it real? We was together for almost three years and you just up and threw it away for a nigga that you was with for like six months before he got locked up. You said you loved me and I believed you. But sending me to jail and taking my money wasn't love. So I wanna know if what we had was real?"

Quitta thought about how to answer his question. Steph had been good to her. Gave her everything she wanted and some. She owed him the truth. "Yeah, it was real. I had real feelings for you, but I never stopped loving Junior. I thought he was my soulmate, so I did whatever I needed to do to be with him. But now that I been with him, I realized that he probably ain't my soulmate. Now I'm just try'na figure out how I'mma raise these kids on my own."

Steph nodded. "I gotta respect you telling the truth, even though it hurt a little. I'mma get out of here. I'll see you around."

"Wait!" Quitta said, stopping him from leaving. "Can we at least be friends?"

Steph looked her in the eyes and shook his head. "We can't be friends, Quitta, because I'm still in love with you. I'mma see you later."

Quitta sat on the toilet and watched him leave. She knew in her heart that she had fucked over a good nigga. Damn.

"Oh my god! Amy! Amy, wake up!" someone was yelling.

Quitta left the bathroom and followed the screams to a bedroom near the back of the house. Amy was laying across the bed foaming at the mouth and another woman was trying to wake her up.

"What the fuck happened!?" Quitta asked.

"Why the hell did you give her the drugs? She's overdosing!"

"I don't know what you talking about. I didn't give her shit," Quitta denied.

The screams brought more people into the room. "What the hell happened?" Megan asked.

"She said Quitta bought her some drugs and now she's overdosing!"

"Shit, I'm calling 911," Megan said, pulling out her phone.

Quitta grabbed Rakisha. "C'mon, girl. We the only Black people in here. Let's go!"

***

They made it back to Rakisha's house safely, but Quitta was worried about the white girl.

"Call Megan back and ask her if Amy okay." Quitta panicked, wishing she didn't buy the drugs.

Rakisha dialed Megan's number again, but it went to voicemail. "She still ain't answering."

Quitta got up from the couch and paced the living room. "I think I should leave. I need to go to a hotel. If she die, they gon' charge me."

"Girl, you tripping," Rakisha said, blowing Quitta's worries off.

"I seen this shit on *Chicago PD*. They can charge the person that sold them the drugs," Quitta said, convinced that she was going to jail.

"Girl, sit yo' ass down and—" Rakisha was saying when someone began banging on the door.

Quitta's eyes grew wide as egg whites. "Shit! That's the police!"

"This is the Lacrosse Police Department! Open the door right now!" a man yelled.

Quitta and Rakisha went into full panic mode and began jumping around, unsure of what to do.

"Open the door right now or we'll break it down!!" the police yelled, banging on the door again.

"Hide in the closet, bitch! Hide in the closet!" Rakisha told Quitta. "Toogie, take the kids upstairs!"

Quitta ran and dove in the closet, covering herself with clothes while Toogie ran upstairs with the kids.

"Open the door right now!" the police yelled again.

Rakisha tip-toed over to the door and unlocked it. The police pushed it open and rushed in, pointing their guns.

"Where is Quitta!?" they demanded, pointing a gun at Rakisha.

"Ahhh!" Rakisha screamed, falling on the ground in terror.

"Where is Quitta?" the cops demanded as they began searching through the house.

"I don't know who that is," Rakisha lied as tears began pouring from her eyes.

"Who is in the house? How many people in here?" the cops asked.

186

"Just me, my kids, and my brothers and sisters. Please don't shoot us!" Rakisha said, getting hysterical.

The cops moved to search the closet while the others went upstairs.

"There's someone in here!" a cop searching the closet yelled. "Get out of there right now before I shoot!"

Quitta stood up slowly, her body shaking with fear and tears pouring down her face. "Please, don't shoot me! I'm pregnant!"

"Get on the ground! Are you Quitta!?" one of the cops yelled as he snatched her from the closet.

"Ouch! My arm!" Quitta yelled as she fell on the ground.

"Is your name Quitta?" the cop asked again.

"No. I'm Shawna," Quitta lied, using her sister's name.

"You fit the description of a woman named Quitta. Show me your ID."

"I don't have an ID," Quitta cried.

"Well, we will have to take you to the station to identify you," the cop said while slapping on the handcuffs.

"Rakisha, call Junior and tell him I need a lawyer!"

***

Quitta sat in the interrogation room biting her bottom lip, legs shaking uncontrollably. She tried to stop crying but couldn't. The life she had known flashed before her eyes, replaced by images of life in jail. She pictured the judge giving her a life sentence, having her baby in a prison hospital, and the guards snatching the baby away. She imagined Mooka calling another woman mama and Junior getting on his knee and proposing to Mooka's new mother.

"Oh, my god!" she cried. "Please get me out of here! Please, God!"

The door opened a few moments later, and a tall and skinny white man walked in. He was clean shaved and wore a blue suit. In one hand was a laptop computer. In the other a McDonald's bag. He eyed Quitta as he sat the computer and food on the table and sat down. "You hungry?" he asked, nodding toward the food.

187

"No. I want a lawyer," Quitta mumbled, doing what Junior told her to do.

He nodded. "Okay. That can be arranged. But do you want to hear what I have to say, or should I leave?"

Quitta wasn't sure how to respond. She wanted to know what was going to happen to her, but she also didn't want to talk herself into some bullshit. Curiosity got the best of her. "What you gotta say?"

"My name is Detective Mark Washington," he said while opening the bag of food and handing Quitta the cheeseburger. "I know that you didn't sell Amy the drugs. I know that you aren't a drug dealer. The problem is, I can't ask Amy who sold her the drugs because she's dead. Megan and Storm say you gave her the drugs. So, as it stands, you're going to be charged with killing Amy unless you can tell me who you got the drugs from."

Quitta's worst nightmare came true. She was about to be charged with murder! Shit. "I want a lawyer," she repeated as more tears welled up in her eyes.

The detective nodded. "I heard you the first time. And that is your right to have a lawyer. But I have more things to say that you probably want to hear. But again, if you want me to leave, I'll go. Do you want to hear what I have to say?" he asked, sounding like he was talking to a kid in kindergarten.

Quitta closed her eyes and shook her head. She didn't know what to do. She was in over her head. "Please, Detective. I didn't kill nobody. You said you know I didn't do it. Why can't I leave?" she cried.

"Because there is more that we need to discuss. Would you like me to show you what I'm talking about?"

Quitta nodded. "Yeah."

He flipped open the laptop and opened a folder. Pictures of Junior, Terrance, Fredo, and a picture of her from the club showed on the screen. The detective blew up each picture one by one. "Do any of these people look familiar to you?"

Quitta felt like she was about to pass out. "I want a lawyer!"

To Be Continued…
A Gangster's Pain 3
Coming Soon

Lock Down Publications and Ca$h Presents assisted
publishing packages.

BASIC PACKAGE $499

Editing

Cover Design

Formatting

UPGRADED PACKAGE $800

Typing

Editing

Cover Design

Formatting

ADVANCE PACKAGE $1,200

Typing

Editing

Cover Design

Formatting

Copyright registration

Proofreading

Upload book to Amazon

LDP SUPREME PACKAGE $1,500

Typing

Editing

Cover Design

Formatting

Copyright registration

Proofreading

Set up Amazon account

Upload book to Amazon

Advertise on LDP Amazon and Facebook page

***Other services available upon request. Additional charges may apply

Lock Down Publications

J-Blunt

P.O. Box 944

Stockbridge, GA 30281-9998

Phone # 470 303-9761

Submission Guideline

Submit the first three chapters of your completed manuscript to ldpsubmissions@gmail.com, subject line: Your book's title. The manuscript must be in a .doc file and sent as an attachment. Document should be in Times New Roman, double spaced and in size 12 font. Also, provide your synopsis and full contact information. If sending multiple submissions, they must each be in a separate email.

Have a story but no way to send it electronically? You can still submit to LDP/Ca$h Presents. Send in the first three chapters, written or typed, of your completed manuscript to:

LDP: Submissions Dept
Po Box 944
Stockbridge, Ga 30281

DO NOT send original manuscript. Must be a duplicate.

Provide your synopsis and a cover letter containing your full contact information.

Thanks for considering LDP and Ca$h Presents.

NEW RELEASES

VICIOIUS LOYALTY 2 by KINGPEN
THE STREETS WILL NEVER CLOSE 3 by K'AJJI
THE MURDER QUEENS by MICHAEL GALLON
THE BIRTH OF A GANGSTER by DELMONT PLAYER
MOB TIES 6 by SAYNOMORE
A GANGSTA'S PAIN 2 by J-BLUNT

Coming Soon from Lock Down Publications/Ca$h Presents

BLOOD OF A BOSS **VI**

SHADOWS OF THE GAME II

TRAP BASTARD II

By **Askari**

LOYAL TO THE GAME **IV**

By **T.J. & Jelissa**

IF TRUE SAVAGE **VIII**

MIDNIGHT CARTEL IV

DOPE BOY MAGIC IV

CITY OF KINGZ III

NIGHTMARE ON SILENT AVE II

THE PLUG OF LIL MEXICO II

By **Chris Green**

BLAST FOR ME **III**

A SAVAGE DOPEBOY III

CUTTHROAT MAFIA III

DUFFLE BAG CARTEL VII

HEARTLESS GOON VI

By **Ghost**

A HUSTLER'S DECEIT III

KILL ZONE II

BAE BELONGS TO ME III

By **Aryanna**

KING OF THE TRAP III

By **T.J. Edwards**

GORILLAZ IN THE BAY V

3X KRAZY III

STRAIGHT BEAST MODE II

De'Kari

KINGPIN KILLAZ IV

STREET KINGS III

PAID IN BLOOD III

CARTEL KILLAZ IV

DOPE GODS III

Hood Rich

SINS OF A HUSTLA II

ASAD

RICH $AVAGE II

By Martell Troublesome Bolden

YAYO V

Bred In The Game 2

S. Allen

CREAM III

THE STREETS WILL TALK II

By Yolanda Moore

SON OF A DOPE FIEND III

HEAVEN GOT A GHETTO II

By Renta

LOYALTY AIN'T PROMISED III

By Keith Williams

I'M NOTHING WITHOUT HIS LOVE II

SINS OF A THUG II

TO THE THUG I LOVED BEFORE II

IN A HUSTLER I TRUST II

By Monet Dragun

QUIET MONEY IV

EXTENDED CLIP III

THUG LIFE IV

By **Trai'Quan**

THE STREETS MADE ME IV

By **Larry D. Wright**

IF YOU CROSS ME ONCE II

By **Anthony Fields**

THE STREETS WILL NEVER CLOSE IV

By **K'ajji**

HARD AND RUTHLESS III

KILLA KOUNTY III

By **Khufu**

MONEY GAME III

By **Smoove Dolla**

JACK BOYS VS DOPE BOYS II

A GANGSTA'S QUR'AN V

COKE GIRLZ II

By **Romell Tukes**

MURDA WAS THE CASE II

Elijah R. Freeman

THE STREETS NEVER LET GO II

By **Robert Baptiste**

AN UNFORESEEN LOVE III

By **Meesha**

KING OF THE TRENCHES III

by **GHOST & TRANAY ADAMS**

MONEY MAFIA II

LOYAL TO THE SOIL III

By **Jibril Williams**

QUEEN OF THE ZOO II

By **Black Migo**

THE BRICK MAN IV

By **King Rio**

J-Blunt

VICIOUS LOYALTY III

By Kingpen

A GANGSTA'S PAIN III

By J-Blunt

CONFESSIONS OF A JACKBOY III

By Nicholas Lock

GRIMEY WAYS II

By Ray Vinci

KING KILLA II

By Vincent "Vitto" Holloway

BETRAYAL OF A THUG II

By Fre$h

THE MURDER QUEENS II

By Michael Gallon

THE BIRTH OF A GANGSTER II

By Delmont Player

Available Now

RESTRAINING ORDER **I & II**

By **CA$H & Coffee**

LOVE KNOWS NO BOUNDARIES **I II & III**

By **Coffee**

RAISED AS A GOON I, II, III & IV

BRED BY THE SLUMS I, II, III

BLAST FOR ME I & II

ROTTEN TO THE CORE I II III

A BRONX TALE I, II, III

DUFFLE BAG CARTEL I II III IV V VI

A Gangsta's Pain 2

HEARTLESS GOON I II III IV V

A SAVAGE DOPEBOY I II

DRUG LORDS I II III

CUTTHROAT MAFIA I II

KING OF THE TRENCHES

By **Ghost**

LAY IT DOWN **I & II**

LAST OF A DYING BREED I II

BLOOD STAINS OF A SHOTTA I & II III

By **Jamaica**

LOYAL TO THE GAME I II III

LIFE OF SIN I, II III

By **TJ & Jelissa**

BLOODY COMMAS I & II

SKI MASK CARTEL I II & III

KING OF NEW YORK I II,III IV V

RISE TO POWER I II III

COKE KINGS I II III IV V

BORN HEARTLESS I II III IV

KING OF THE TRAP I II

By **T.J. Edwards**

IF LOVING HIM IS WRONG…I & II

LOVE ME EVEN WHEN IT HURTS I II III

By **Jelissa**

WHEN THE STREETS CLAP BACK I & II III

THE HEART OF A SAVAGE I II III

MONEY MAFIA

LOYAL TO THE SOIL I II

By **Jibril Williams**

A DISTINGUISHED THUG STOLE MY HEART I II & III

J-Blunt

LOVE SHOULDN'T HURT I II III IV

RENEGADE BOYS I II III IV

PAID IN KARMA I II III

SAVAGE STORMS I II III

AN UNFORESEEN LOVE I II

By **Meesha**

A GANGSTER'S CODE I &, II III

A GANGSTER'S SYN I II III

THE SAVAGE LIFE I II III

CHAINED TO THE STREETS I II III

BLOOD ON THE MONEY I II III

A GANGSTA'S PAIN I II

By J-Blunt

PUSH IT TO THE LIMIT

By **Bre' Hayes**

BLOOD OF A BOSS **I, II, III, IV, V**

SHADOWS OF THE GAME

TRAP BASTARD

By **Askari**

THE STREETS BLEED MURDER **I, II & III**

THE HEART OF A GANGSTA I II& III

By **Jerry Jackson**

CUM FOR ME I II III IV V VI VII VIII

An **LDP Erotica Collaboration**

BRIDE OF A HUSTLA **I II & II**

THE FETTI GIRLS **I, II& III**

CORRUPTED BY A GANGSTA I, II III, IV

BLINDED BY HIS LOVE

THE PRICE YOU PAY FOR LOVE I, II ,III

DOPE GIRL MAGIC I II III

A Gangsta's Pain 2

By **Destiny Skai**
WHEN A GOOD GIRL GOES BAD
By **Adrienne**
THE COST OF LOYALTY I II III
By Kweli
A GANGSTER'S REVENGE **I II III & IV**
THE BOSS MAN'S DAUGHTERS I II III IV V
A SAVAGE LOVE **I & II**
BAE BELONGS TO ME I II
A HUSTLER'S DECEIT I, II, III
WHAT BAD BITCHES DO I, II, III
SOUL OF A MONSTER I II III
KILL ZONE
A DOPE BOY'S QUEEN I II III
By **Aryanna**
A KINGPIN'S AMBITON
A KINGPIN'S AMBITION **II**
I MURDER FOR THE DOUGH
By **Ambitious**
TRUE SAVAGE I II III IV V VI VII
DOPE BOY MAGIC I, II, III
MIDNIGHT CARTEL I II III
CITY OF KINGZ I II
NIGHTMARE ON SILENT AVE
THE PLUG OF LIL MEXICO II

By **Chris Green**
A DOPEBOY'S PRAYER
By **Eddie "Wolf" Lee**
THE KING CARTEL **I, II & III**

J-Blunt

By **Frank Gresham**

THESE NIGGAS AIN'T LOYAL **I, II & III**

By **Nikki Tee**

GANGSTA SHYT **I II &III**

By **CATO**

THE ULTIMATE BETRAYAL

By **Phoenix**

BOSS'N UP **I , II & III**

By **Royal Nicole**

I LOVE YOU TO DEATH

By **Destiny J**

I RIDE FOR MY HITTA

I STILL RIDE FOR MY HITTA

By **Misty Holt**

LOVE & CHASIN' PAPER

By **Qay Crockett**

TO DIE IN VAIN

SINS OF A HUSTLA

By **ASAD**

BROOKLYN HUSTLAZ

By **Boogsy Morina**

BROOKLYN ON LOCK I & II

By **Sonovia**

GANGSTA CITY

By **Teddy Duke**

A DRUG KING AND HIS DIAMOND I & II III

A DOPEMAN'S RICHES

HER MAN, MINE'S TOO I, II

CASH MONEY HO'S

THE WIFEY I USED TO BE I II

A Gangsta's Pain 2

By Nicole Goosby
TRAPHOUSE KING **I II & III**
KINGPIN KILLAZ I II III
STREET KINGS I II
PAID IN BLOOD **I II**
CARTEL KILLAZ I II III
DOPE GODS I II
By **Hood Rich**
LIPSTICK KILLAH **I, II, III**
CRIME OF PASSION I II & III
FRIEND OR FOE I II III
By **Mimi**
STEADY MOBBN' **I, II, III**
THE STREETS STAINED MY SOUL I II III
By **Marcellus Allen**
WHO SHOT YA **I, II, III**
SON OF A DOPE FIEND I II
HEAVEN GOT A GHETTO
Renta
GORILLAZ IN THE BAY **I II III IV**
TEARS OF A GANGSTA I II
3X KRAZY I II
STRAIGHT BEAST MODE
DE'KARI
TRIGGADALE I II III
MURDAROBER WAS THE CASE
Elijah R. Freeman
GOD BLESS THE TRAPPERS I, II, III
THESE SCANDALOUS STREETS I, II, III
FEAR MY GANGSTA I, II, III IV, V

J-Blunt

THESE STREETS DON'T LOVE NOBODY I, II

BURY ME A G I, II, III, IV, V

A GANGSTA'S EMPIRE I, II, III, IV

THE DOPEMAN'S BODYGAURD I II

THE REALEST KILLAZ I II III

THE LAST OF THE OGS I II III

Tranay Adams

THE STREETS ARE CALLING

Duquie Wilson

MARRIED TO A BOSS I II III

By Destiny Skai & Chris Green

KINGZ OF THE GAME I II III IV V VI

Playa Ray

SLAUGHTER GANG I II III

RUTHLESS HEART I II III

By Willie Slaughter

FUK SHYT

By Blakk Diamond

DON'T F#CK WITH MY HEART I II

By Linnea

ADDICTED TO THE DRAMA I II III

IN THE ARM OF HIS BOSS II

By Jamila

YAYO I II III IV

A SHOOTER'S AMBITION I II

BRED IN THE GAME

By S. Allen

TRAP GOD I II III

RICH $AVAGE

MONEY IN THE GRAVE I II III

204

A Gangsta's Pain 2

By Martell Troublesome Bolden
FOREVER GANGSTA
GLOCKS ON SATIN SHEETS I II
By Adrian Dulan
TOE TAGZ I II III IV
LEVELS TO THIS SHYT I II
By Ah'Million
KINGPIN DREAMS I II III
By Paper Boi Rari
CONFESSIONS OF A GANGSTA I II III IV
CONFESSIONS OF A JACKBOY I II
By Nicholas Lock
I'M NOTHING WITHOUT HIS LOVE
SINS OF A THUG
TO THE THUG I LOVED BEFORE
A GANGSTA SAVED XMAS
IN A HUSTLER I TRUST
By Monet Dragun
CAUGHT UP IN THE LIFE I II III
THE STREETS NEVER LET GO
By Robert Baptiste
NEW TO THE GAME I II III
MONEY, MURDER & MEMORIES I II III
By Malik D. Rice
LIFE OF A SAVAGE I II III
A GANGSTA'S QUR'AN I II III IV
MURDA SEASON I II III
GANGLAND CARTEL I II III
CHI'RAQ GANGSTAS I II III
KILLERS ON ELM STREET I II III

J-Blunt

JACK BOYZ N DA BRONX I II III

A DOPEBOY'S DREAM I II III

JACK BOYS VS DOPE BOYS

COKE GIRLZ

By Romell Tukes

LOYALTY AIN'T PROMISED I II

By Keith Williams

QUIET MONEY I II III

THUG LIFE I II III

EXTENDED CLIP I II

By **Trai'Quan**

THE STREETS MADE ME I II III

By **Larry D. Wright**

THE ULTIMATE SACRIFICE I, II, III, IV, V, VI

KHADIFI

IF YOU CROSS ME ONCE

ANGEL I II

IN THE BLINK OF AN EYE

By **Anthony Fields**

THE LIFE OF A HOOD STAR

By Ca$h & Rashia Wilson

THE STREETS WILL NEVER CLOSE I II III

By K'ajji

CREAM I II

THE STREETS WILL TALK

By Yolanda Moore

NIGHTMARES OF A HUSTLA I II III

By King Dream

CONCRETE KILLA I II

VICIOUS LOYALTY I II

A Gangsta's Pain 2

By Kingpen

HARD AND RUTHLESS I II

MOB TOWN 251

THE BILLIONAIRE BENTLEYS I II III

By Von Diesel

GHOST MOB

Stilloan Robinson

MOB TIES I II III IV V VI

By SayNoMore

BODYMORE MURDERLAND I II III

THE BIRTH OF A GANGSTER

By Delmont Player

FOR THE LOVE OF A BOSS

By C. D. Blue

MOBBED UP I II III IV

THE BRICK MAN I II III

THE COCAINE PRINCESS I II III IV V

By King Rio

KILLA KOUNTY I II III

By Khufu

MONEY GAME I II

By Smoove Dolla

A GANGSTA'S KARMA I II

By FLAME

KING OF THE TRENCHES I II

by **GHOST & TRANAY ADAMS**

QUEEN OF THE ZOO

By **Black Migo**

GRIMEY WAYS

By Ray Vinci

XMAS WITH AN ATL SHOOTER

By Ca$h & Destiny Skai

KING KILLA

By Vincent "Vitto" Holloway

BETRAYAL OF A THUG

By Fre$h

THE MURDER QUEENS

By Michael Gallon

BOOKS BY LDP'S CEO, CA$H

TRUST IN NO MAN

TRUST IN NO MAN 2

TRUST IN NO MAN 3

BONDED BY BLOOD

SHORTY GOT A THUG

THUGS CRY

THUGS CRY 2

THUGS CRY 3

TRUST NO BITCH

TRUST NO BITCH 2

TRUST NO BITCH 3

TIL MY CASKET DROPS

RESTRAINING ORDER

RESTRAINING ORDER 2

IN LOVE WITH A CONVICT

LIFE OF A HOOD STAR

XMAS WITH AN ATL SHOOTER

J-Blunt